Murder and Pink Blossoms

… A Ladies-of-a-Certain-Age Mystery…

Elizabeth J. Wheeler

November 2019

LCA Press Grand Junction, Colorado
www.ladiesofacertainage.com

Cover Designer: Joyce Cerritti

THIS BOOK IS DEDICATED TO:

Henry John Wind
The most courageous and kind person I know

And to
Oscar Francis Wind and Lucille Rose Wind
His loving older brother and twin sister

ACKNOWLEDGEMENTS

I never dreamed I would become a mystery writer. When this story bombarded me one summer day in my backyard, I knew I had to write the mystery. Although I have written a lot in my life, including news releases, speeches, newspaper columns, magazine articles, memoirs, advertising copy, marketing communications, blogs, and several non-fiction books, I had not delved into fiction writing since high school. I am deeply indebted to many writers and those who reviewed various renditions of this book. Believe me, it was quite a leap for me to jump across the bridge from fact to fantasy.

These wonderful people gave me so much of their time, expertise and encouragement: Richard Wohlgenant, Jane and Ivan Cardenas, Sandy Dorr, Virginia Jensen, Chris Kanaly, Jane Miller, the late Joe Skinner, John Lynch, John Lallement, Judy and Bill Thompson, Marie Arelsgaatd, Connie Solomon, Beth Yoder Washington, Suzanne Young, and Bonnie McCune. Thank you.

Also, I want to thank all of the men and women who shared their lives with me and gave me support in open Alcoholics Anonymous and Al-Anon meetings I have attended. I came to realize what motivates people besides money, is matters of the heart.

CHAPTER ONE
BODY IN THE ALLEY
...VERDICT PRIOR TO INVESTIGATION...

Ellen woke up from a dream about fudge. No wonder, she thought, as she snuggled back under the covers. My whole house smells of the batch of candy I made last night. But, I really can't take a snooze. There is so much to do in just a little over two weeks before the Pink Blossoms Garden and Neighborhood Tour in honor of Mamie Eisenhower.

She put on her robe, let her Airedale Terrier, Buttercup, out the back door and walked down the stairs to the basement to fill up her bowl with dog food. Her tuxedo cat, Sweetie Pie, scampered down the stairs with her. She fed both animals, cleaned the cat box, and then, went back upstairs and let Buttercup in.

Shivering from the chilly April air coming in through the back door, Ellen scurried to her room, threw on a pair of black yoga pants, a long sleeve t-shirt, her down vest, wool socks and clogs and then hurried to the kitchen, made coffee and filled her bowl with cereal and fruit. She grabbed her notebook and daily reader from the 12-Step program she had belonged to for over 25 years. She wrote her daily letter to the "Universe," asking for help and guidance that day.

Ellen thought, oh, my! It's almost 6:45 a.m. Before Axle's workers start clogging up the alley, I've got to put my coat on, get to the garage and unlock the chain to the alley I put up last night, and drive to yoga.

She put on her black pea coat, gloves and a hat, gave Buttercup a kiss on her head, and said, "Goodbye,

1

Sweetie Pie wherever you are."

Ellen bolted out the backdoor, locked it and its heavy-duty security screen door and ran to her garage. Finding the key to the lock she had put on the thick yellow chain strewn between a large eye hook screwed into one side of her garage and her neighbor's chain link fence, she opened the garage door to the driveway.

As the door opened, Ellen noticed a stream of red running down part of her driveway towards the alley and slowly dripping into a crevice, known to her and her neighbors as the "fishing hole." She traced it back to the chain and screamed.

The body of a small man with dark hair and swarthy skin was draped over the thick yellow chain. Part of his head had been severed, dangling from a thin sinew, and sticking out his butt was a long, thick wooden pole, which Ellen recognized as a tree pruner used to saw tall branches. He wore a green Axle Tree Service shirt. Blood was everywhere. His corpse swung to and fro on the chain, his black hair sweeping through great gobs of thick blood, producing a modernistic painting on the cement.

Shaking almost uncontrollably, Ellen ran back into the garage, got in her car, fumbled in her purse for her phone and called 9-1-1.

"Englewood Police Department. How can I help you?" the dispatcher asked.

"There's a dead man in my alley that has been brutally killed!"

"How do you know he is dead?"

"His head is almost off. There is blood everywhere. There is a tree pole sticking from his butt."

"Who am I speaking to?"

"Ellen Lane."

"What is the address? I'll have police there right away,"

"3136 Emerald Street."

"Thank you. Help is on the way. Where are you?"

"I'm in my car in my garage. "

"Stay inside, lock your doors and close the garage door. I will have an officer call you at this number as soon as police arrive."

Within minutes, the cops arrived.

Hearing the sirens, Axle Kutz, who lived directly behind Ellen, ran out of his house to the alley and turned ashen when he saw the dead man. *Oh, no*, he thought. I will be accused of this murder too, just like the murder of my parents. But this time, there is no time to flee.

Neighbors, Sam and Nancy, hurried down the alley. Brent's new wife showed up too, and other neighbors began to gather as the sirens shrilled. Many of them hopped out of their cars as they were driving down the alley, as part of their daily commute to work. Even old Annie in her wool coat and knit hat, using her cane, came to watch. An ambulance appeared. Axle's workers started arriving. Approaching the alley, trash trucks came to a screeching halt when they saw the emergency lights and people gathered.

Captain Mark McCoy showed up, taking charge of the scene.

"Well, well, well, Axle, looks like one of your guys got stiffed in the alley. Know his name? By the color of his skin, we don't think he has been dead very long." He grabbed Axle by his large bicep and pulled him close to the dead man.

Axle threw up. He recognized the guy because he had had a fight with him the day before over not getting his pay on time. He had told him to come back the next day to work and to collect his pay.

Ellen's phone rang. "Ms. Lane, this is Officer

Dan Green. We are in the alley and have secured it. Please unlock your garage door, and I will escort you into your house."

She opened the door with her remote and saw a tall slender cop with sandy hair and washed-out blue eyes. Green opened Ellen's car door and helped the shaking older woman out of her car. When they got to the driveway, Ellen heard Axle blurt out, "I think the guy's name is Hector Hernandez!"

"Get into the car, Axle. Because you are a person of interest, I need you to come down to the station to answer some questions about this death," McCoy stated.

The captain then tipped his hat to Annie. "I hope, Miss Annie, you can help us like you helped us with the drug gang a couple of years ago."

.

CHAPTER TWO
COPS INTERROGATE ELLEN IN HER KITCHEN
...DASHED HOPES AND BROKEN DREAMS...

"Although my dog, Buttercup, is big, she won't hurt you," Ellen said to Officer Green as he opened the back door for her. After calming her dog down, she collapsed into one of her kitchen chairs.

Gathering herself and remembering her manners, the always considerate Ellen asked Green, "Can I make you a cup of coffee?"

"That is very kind of you, but I've already had lots of coffee this morn," Green stated, amazed people who had witnessed something terrible almost always offered him something to drink before he sat down with them to talk.

"Ok. Well, while I am making myself a cup, maybe you would like a piece of fudge," Ellen said, putting a plate down on her round white Formica table, which looked like it had always been in the little kitchen nook.

Sitting in one of the black chairs from the same time period, Green took a look around Ellen's kitchen. It seemed like it had recently been remodeled, with new white cabinets and one of those white apron sinks. Since the flooring was not dirty looking and scuffed, the black and white linoleum squares appeared to be new too, even though Green knew linoleum generally on the floors of kitchens built in the 1950s. His grandmother had a kitchen kind of like this in her ranch-style home, which was built shortly after WWII.

Ellen sat down and told Green, "I made this fudge last night, using Mamie Doud Eisenhower's famous recipe. We're going to be selling fudge in a couple of weeks at the Pink Blossoms Garden and Neighborhood Tour we are having in honor of Mamie. I bring a batch of it to potential sponsors when we meet with them."

She went on, "You know, she grew up in Denver, and we all knew she loved the color pink and fudge. When I was a kid, everyone planted pink crabapple trees in the new neighborhoods sprouting up like crabgrass after WWII. Many of the soldiers stationed at Fitzsimons Army Base or Lowry Army Air Base fell in love with this area. They appreciated the dry climate and view of the nearby mountains. So when the war was over, they settled here and the population boomed."

"Oh," Green said. "Maybe that is why my mom's favorite Christmas ornament is pink. She hangs it each year. She has had it since she was a little girl."

"How long have you lived here, Ms. Lane, and why are you making fudge for a neighborhood tour?" Green asked.

"I've only lived here a couple of years, and the money we raise from selling fudge will help us buy playground equipment for Englewood schools."

The cop went on, "What brought you to this neighborhood, Ms. Lane?"

"Well, after retiring a couple of years ago, I needed to downsize from my big house on a corner lot, to boot! It was in what used to be called 'Old North Denver.' Also, I wanted to live closer to what little family I have. So my cousin, Murphy, who is a realtor, and I started looking for a new house for me. You know the Denver-area's market is really hot, so we knew my house would sell quickly. I put it on the market and thank goodness, Murph and I found this one right away. My big house sold in two days!"

Green rubbed his chin as if he was pondering the next question. "That must have been quite a change for you. That neighborhood is very different from Olde Englewood. North Denver has experienced quite resurgence in the past couple of years. I understand it is now one of Denver's so-called hottest markets. How old was your house?"

"Yes, it was quite a change for me. My big beautiful brick Craftsman was close to 100-years-old. There are many neat shops in the area, which I could walk to. This house had been a rental for 10 years or so. When I first saw it, I thought it had little character. The siding was white and the trim was gray. Obviously, all the houses on this side of the street were built by the same builder. The only variation was in placement of the porch. They looked like a clump of Monopoly houses sitting on several of the low-cost properties on the Monopoly board."

Green helped himself to another piece of fudge, and Ellen grabbed one before going on.

"But Murph and I could tell this house was solidly built, and we knew the owners, who had inherited the house from their grandparents, had redone the floors and completely painted it inside and out. Another advantage of the house was its living room's large picture window, which faces west. The view of the mountains, especially when the sun is setting, is spectacular. All of the windows are wood, not aluminum, which became very popular soon after this house was built. Aluminum windows leak air, making the house cold in the winter and hot in the summer."

Buttercup came over to Ellen's side and looked up at her owner.

"No, Buttercup, chocolate is not good for dogs. Fortunately for Buttercup, the backyard is about as big as our former yard. At 80 pounds or so, it's important for big Buttercup to have a yard to run around in. Besides the backyard and the home being solidly well built, I loved the two large Golden Sunburst Locust trees in the front yard and the archways to the upstairs and downstairs bedrooms. But the kitchen, unlike my previous one, needed to be redone and the house required new electrical service for all the things we do today requiring electricity. The owners worked with me on the price and also, I got a nice profit on my old house. So, I upgraded the electrical system, painted the house a cheery yellow, put up black shutters, and remodeled the kitchen, keeping the 1950s appearance as much as possible."

She took several deep gulps of the strong, dark coffee. A knock on her back door brought Ellen back to the present moment. Buttercup started barking ferociously.

Ellen jumped out of her kitchen chair, but Green held up a hand to stop her as he strode towards the door and opened it. An older cop stood there. He was big and hefty, with sandy hair turning gray in his late 50s. "Ms. Lane, this is Captain Mark McCoy," Green stated when he introduced the cop to Ellen.

"Captain McCoy, are you the same Mark McCoy I have been emailing to bitch about this alley and trash companies?" Ellen asked.

"Well, yes, ma'am, I am. There was a job with Englewood Police in code enforcement, which I thought would be far less stressful than the investigator position I had in Denver. Me and the Misses have lived near Englewood for some time and thought this job would get us to retirement."

"But you're doing detective work now?" Ellen asked.

Looking not too pleased, McCoy answered Ellen's question. "Oh, for the past year or so,

Englewood has experienced increased crime, particularly drug-related crime, and the department head asked me to step in 'for a little while' and take over investigations after my predecessor had a heart attack."

"I see, Captain McCoy. Would you like a cup of coffee and a piece of fudge?" Ellen asked.

"Why, yes, ma'am. That is very kind of you. Please feel free to call me McCoy." The captain sat down at the kitchen table.

"Ms. Lane, I don't know if you got a good look at the deceased, but if you did, did you recognize him?"

"No, he looked like many of Axle's workers and had the company green shirt on they all wear." Please call me Ellen."

"Well, well, well, Ellen, did you ever expect such an awful thing would happen in your neighborhood? I know you have had your difficulties with Axle and his tree company. What can you tell us about all this?"

"No, I certainly did not expect to ever see a dead man, let alone one on my property. It's been bad enough with Axle Kutz and his workers and all those trash companies, trying to go down this weird shaped alley," she said, handing McCoy a cup of freshly made coffee and grabbing her own cup. "Axle has a temper, for sure. But I have never heard him raise his voice to any of his workers. The workers don't stick with him very long, you know. I've never seen him drink or smoke, for that matter, and he works all the time. Sam, my neighbor who lives two doors to the north of me, told me his son Keith tried working for Axle during a school break. Axle never paid him even though Axle promised he would get to an ATM that very day and get the money. Sam did tell me 'Ms. Mouse,' that's what we call the woman who lived with her little daughter and Axle, left because he abused her."

After swallowing another big gulp of coffee, McCoy said, "Well, the looks of the cut on Hector's neck seems to have come from an alligator lopper. That piece of equipment is used to cut big limbs. It's a specialty tool. Pole tree loppers are more common, but the size of the one extending from his buttocks leads me to believe it is a tool for commercial use. The deceased is small, probably only outweighing you by 20 or 30 pounds. But I don't think you are strong enough to wield that equipment."

"What? You considered me as a possible murderer?" She looked at McCoy and then at Green. "I did not realize that Officer Green would be recording my conversation with you."

"We always question the person who finds the body you know, Ellen. Officer Green is writing down some notes, but believe me, he is not recording everything. If we thought you were a person of interest, I would ask you to come to police headquarters. At this point we are trying to get background information. So I am wondering if the victim looks at all familiar to you?"

"Seems like I saw him in the alley before, but there are so many of them. I am not really sure. I have the impression Axle hires many Hispanics, but also he hires many other ethnicities and both sexes."

"Were any of your neighbors in the alley when you came out, Ellen?"

"No, most of them leave for work shortly after Axle and his crew leave. The guy next door rarely works, and his live-in girl friend goes to work about 9. Besides, they don't have a garage. I never see them in the alley. The garages were built a number of years after these homes were constructed in the early 1950s. That is why they are all 2-car garages. Back in the early 50s, if a garage was built with a house, it was one-car for the single family vehicle. So, my neighbors on the south leave through the front door and park their vehicles on the street. From what I heard you say this morning when I was sitting in my car in the garage, I think you might know my other next-door neighbor, Annie?"

"Yes. That is true, Ellen. A couple of years ago a drug gang was very active in these parts. Annie saw them make a deal in the alley and called the police. Without her seeing that handoff, we would have never been able to make an arrest. She has good eyes and lots of time, that's for sure. Who else, Ellen, could have seen something?"

"Well, Sam and his wife and their son have a paper route. But they leave very early, around 4 a.m. I think, and don't return until after I have left for my yoga class. The guy who lives across the alley from Sam I don't know, and I hardly ever see him. The first Thanksgiving I was here I might have seen him – at least some guy that is –with a long rifle pointed at a tree between his house and Axle's. He just stood there, pointing his gun. But I wondered what he was aiming at. The scores of squirrels in the neighborhood are real pests, but it did not make sense someone would use such a big gun to kill something so small. He was a big man, too. As big as Axle, maybe bigger. I thought perhaps he was aiming at the numerous sparrow hawks which live around here. I don't know much about guns, but it seemed too big for hawks. A coyote? Could a coyote climb a tree, I wondered. I doubted that, though I have heard they can get up part of a tree if the branches are accommodating. We have lots of fox here, but I think they are red foxes, not gray ones. I know in parts of Colorado foxes do climb trees, but I believe they are gray foxes. Maybe the man had Post Traumatic Stress Disorder, PTSD. Who knows?"

McCoy switched the conversation from

neighbors to trees and asked Ellen, "Anyone else around here astute about trees? I remember sending an inspector out to your house on a complaint from your neighbor to the south. What's his name, again? "

"My neighbor Kelly thought I planted my crabapple tree on his property and called in a complaint! I planted it there to block his filthy dirty window, which sports all those empty liquor bottles. Your guy who came out was well over 7- foot."

"Good cop. His name is Herbert Dahl. He's not quite 7 feet. He's just a little over 6-feet, 11 inches."

Ellen and the cops laughed. She got up, grabbed the coffee pot, and asked McCoy if he wanted more. After sitting back down, she went on, "Herbert thought I might have planted it on the gas line. I showed him where the property and gas lines were located because I had to have them marked in order to get a fence permit. He laughed and said Kelly was supposed to meet him here. Well, Kelly wasn't there, and Herbert was a little ticked."

"Hmmm, Ellen, so this was your only tree issue with Kelly?"

"Nope. The first one was his tree limb over my kitchen roof and not offering to pay for its removal."

"Oh, who did cut it down?"

Ellen replied, "Verdant Tree Company. They've been in business for over 100 years, and I had used them at my former house. I contacted them to trim the locusts in the front. Fortunately, the afternoon they came out to give me a bid, I had just picked up my mail and saw an envelope from the insurance company. To my surprise the letter stated that unless the large limb, which hung over the kitchen roof from my neighbor's tree was removed, this national insurance company, who has been my insurance company for over 30 years -- mind you -- would not insure my roof from damage.

Just then, a young man strode up to me. He reeked of alcohol and cigarettes. A long grayish beard hung from the edge of his chin. He reminded me of the Devil incarnate and seemed to be going prematurely gray. He was carrying a large mug. When he extended his hand, the jostling motion caused the golden contents of the mug to splash all over me, like a tidal wave, which had reached shore. I retracted from the splashing beer."

Ellen chuckled at the memory and drank more coffee before continuing her story.

"He said, 'Oh, sorry about that. I am Kelly, your neighbor. Should have come over earlier to meet you.'"

I replied, "Well, it's fortunate to meet you now, Kelly. The Verdant Tree Company is here today to decide how to trim my trees, and I just received this letter from my insurance company, which states the branch from your tree must be cut back so it does not hang over my roof, or they won't insure my house. Kelly snatched the letter out of my hand and said to me, 'Oh, let me look at that letter. It is from the same insurance company I have. No worries. You don't have to do anything for a couple of months.'"

Leaning back in her chair, Ellen continued, "I told Kelly, since the tree company is here, let's see what we are looking at. Then, the tree man came over and said it would be $100 to remove the branch if they were already on the property trimming trees. I saw Kelly flinch and knew he would never assume financial responsibility for the tree. What I saw in front of me was an alcoholic. I became keenly aware of the state of his property: brown grass, weeds everywhere and a home needing to be painted, all indications to me of his cunning and baffling disease. So since I had experienced the dashed hopes and broken dreams as the former wife of an alcoholic, I told the company I'd pay for the branch. Kelly said that would be just fine with him and trudged back to his house."

"Mmmm. That's quite a story, Ellen. Any other trees on his property that have given you concern?"

"Every now and then branches still fall off of that tree into my backyard, and the tree in the back of Kelly's property sheds branches on my driveway. But the big guy who is frequently there – he might be Kelly's brother, but I am not sure - trimmed up those trees one day."

Just then, Ellen's front door opened and a high-pitched, worried female voice said, "Hey, lady, are you alright?"

Buttercup bounded from under the kitchen table where she had been laying near her owner's legs to the door. Ellen quickly pushed her chair back. McCoy pushed her back down and Green put his hand on his gun.

"Oh, no, please," Ellen stated. "That's my cousin, Murph."

Ellen jumped up, and she and Murph embraced. Both had tears in their eyes.

"Oh, Murph, the most awful thing has happened. A man was murdered in my driveway, and I don't know if anyone will feel safe to come to our tour."

After a couple of moments, Ellen said, "Let me introduce you to the policemen investigating the case. Captain Mark McCoy and Officer Dan Green, this is my cousin Mary Mahoney. Her nickname is Murphy. Both of her parents were of Irish descent, so they gave their red-haired baby girl that name. We have called her that all these years."

Dan Green walked towards Murph and said, "Actually, Ms. Lane, Ms. Mahoney and I met some years ago. She sold my wife and me our first house."

"That's right, Ellen," and Murph shook Green's hand and told him with a grin on her face, "Ellen and I have always been close, but I must say she can be a little rude to her elders at times. After all, I am six months older even though I am a couple inches shorter, weigh 95 pounds to her 120, and am much better looking, particularly because I have brilliant red hair! We have had all sorts of adventures since we met as infants in the late 1940s. Currently, we are working on a tour of this great neighborhood, which may not happen since Ellen told me she found a body in her driveway."

McCoy's phone rang. "McCoy here. Oh, I see. We'll be right out."

"Well, thank you, Ellen, and also for the coffee and the fudge. It is nice to meet you, Ms. Mahoney. Officer Green and I need to leave now. We've been called by our investigation team looking for evidence in the alley."

On his way out, McCoy noticed a note on Ellen's counter near a plate of fudge and the recipe. The note read: Barbara Evans, Santa Fe and Mississippi, 2 p.m. Strange, McCoy thought, isn't that the address of the Teasing Tigress, Denver's famous strip club?

CHAPTER THREE
A LITTLE COMFORT FROM A COUSIN
....SUIT UP AND SHOW UP....

After the cops left, Ellen collapsed on her couch, put her head in her hands and wept. Buttercup immediately sat by her legs. Sweetie Pie jumped in her lap, and her cousin rushed to her side.

"Oh, Murph, it was just awful. That poor man. His head dangling in a pool of blood. His body draped over the yellow chain. Thank God I had that chain link fence taken down, or I might have seen him murdered from my back kitchen window!"

"Dear, dear, dear. You have seen something awful," Murph said, patting her hand. "You know, Ellen, you have always been so strong. I have seen you in really tough media interviews and hard times with your ex-husband and children. You always get through it so cool, calm and collected. I am so glad to see you finally break down. Just cry, dear lady."

After a while, Ellen blew her nose and headed to her bathroom. Murph went to the kitchen and put a cup of water in the microwave for some tea.

When Ellen returned to the couch, Murph gently took her hand and said, "How about some tea, sweetie? I've got some made for both of us. Let's go in the kitchen."

After sitting down at her white table in the kitchen nook and taking a couple of sips of tea, Ellen collected herself. "Oh, Murph, I know this has been a trauma for me. Yes, you are right. I do somehow pull myself up and then go to pieces after it is all over. I don't want anyone to see me upset. It's a very private thing for me. You know crying or showing any emotion

16

at all was not allowed in my family growing up. As an adult, I learned I could no longer hold it all inside or it would come back and bite me in the butt! That's why when I was in my thirties I went into therapy for a couple of years. I now know - at some point - I have to deal with all of my feelings. I know something this traumatic is going to take some time to get over. I am so glad you are here. The tea is wonderful."

Sweetie Pie meandered out of the living room and jumped on the kitchen counter to look out the window above the sink. Ellen saw her, clapped her hands and got up to take the cat off the counter. She put Sweetie Pie on her lap and then continued telling Murph, "You know, something else I learned is there is nothing like getting busy to help me go on. So many times, I had to suit up and show up – as they say – after a horrific fight with my ex-husband, and I was due at work or needed to get our kids someplace. What senseless fights I had with my inebriated husband. I know my poor kids were affected by all of that."

"Yes, I went through a lot of that too," Murph said. "After all, we come from the same stock!"

"You know, Murph, I'm going to play in a golf tournament on the western slope the week after the tour. You could come and join me if you like. It is so peaceful and beautiful there. I love driving over the Colorado National Monument because it always replenishes my soul. We could stop on the way home, and you could go fishing in your favorite stream, the Frying Pan River. I love that name. While you fish, I'll read and do some knitting."

The cousins sat in silence for a couple of minutes and then looked at each other. Both of them blurted out, "We've got to find the murderer soon so the tour can go on and we can go play!" They both started to laugh.

They left the cozy kitchen nook and went into the living room. Ellen sat down on her couch and picked up her knitting. Murph plopped herself down in an oak rocking chair, which had been in their family for decades.

"I can tell you, Murph, I just don't think Axle did it. He's used to gypping people. I think he uses his size and loud words to intimidate people. I know. He has scared the heck out of me a couple of times when we have had altercations in the alley. I think it was even harder for him to argue with me because he is used to frightening women and having them cow down to him. Remember my dad was a big man too, and often picked on me. He one time told me, 'Ellen, you are like a young colt, and I can't break your spirit.' My poor dad had a horrible life, but somehow climbed the corporate ladder. So, I think big men like Axle and my dad often use their size to threaten people. They don't have the social skills to negotiate well. Hector would have had to do something really, really horrible for Axle to kill him. After all, we know Axle was known for not always paying people. If he got mad because Hector confronted him about not getting paid, that would not be anything out of the ordinary for Axle."

"Mmmm. I thought you told me the woman and cute little girl who lived with him left because he abused her. Seems so strange he doesn't have a building and a garage to operate his business out of. I wonder why that is. Or maybe he is into selling drugs. You know, Ellen, you said one time Annie next door told you how she saw a drug deal go down in the alley. Maybe the drug gang is back or another one has taken over, and they have decided to work with Axle. A tree trimming company could be a perfect cover up. What do you think?"

Ellen wound the pink glittery yarn around both

knitting needles, stabbed the needles in the ball of yarn, and put the project in her lap. "Well, drugs are always a possibility. You don't think of it much in this quiet neighborhood. Olde Englewood is not a wealthy area, but we certainly are close to affluent ones in other parts of Englewood, and nearby south Denver and Littleton. I guess you don't have to be rich to buy drugs, but my friends who have addicted spouses and children are fairly well off. So that is why I always think you need money to buy them. We do have three hospitals near my home: Swedish, Porter and Craig are just blocks away. Recently a nurse got busted for stealing some really potent stuff from Swedish. Of course, now that pot is legal, it seems every other store on Broadway sells it. I can see why this alley would be a great location for dealers of pot and all the other stuff. It seems so tucked away in houses and trees because of the funny access, not the usual run from one avenue to another a block away. It is hard to locate because one access is on a typical avenue, but the other comes out at a street. It probably would be good for dealers in another sense because they can make a speedy getaway on nearby Highway 285. But why would they kill Hector, Murph?"

"I don't know, Ellen. It's easy to blame Axle since he had a shouting match with Hector just the other day. But maybe Hector was somehow connected to drugs, and the fight with Axle over pay was just that. Maybe Hector was also working for Axle in addition to his drug work. By the way, are you knitting one of those darling little nineteen fifties evening bags for the women on the committee who are helping us with the tour?"

"Yes. I found this pattern from the nineteen fifties, and it is such fun to knit. I'm glad they don't take much time since I am making seven of them. But I did have to make them bigger since women now generally carry a cell phone, car keys and lipstick. Back then, the purse pattern was big enough for a tube of lipstick and a compact. They did not go out alone, you know. Men drove to where they were going as a couple. I bet Annie next door and the lady who originally owned this house had one similar to it. Can you imagine us owning such a thing, let alone using it for a special date?"

"Oh, heavens no. But back to drugs, didn't you tell me you suspected the guy next door – the creepy one with the creepy girlfriend – was making meth or something? What do you call her?"

"Oh, I call her 'Yah-Yah Girl.' I know that is probably not nice to call her that, but I really don't know her name even after living here for several years. I've never ever talked to her. We do wave when we see each other. Murph, when you have been looking out my living room window, haven't you seen her getting home from work, lumbering out of her big dirty banged-up black SUV, wearing what she wears all the time: A tight black chemise, black capris and black wedge sandals?"

"Oh, yes, I remember now. Her black hair is tied up in an artful do. What's a real kick is her belly hanging over the elastic waistband of the capris and her big boobs jostling underneath the chemise. I remember how – shall we say - 'she alights, like a moose' - from her vehicle with cell phone in one hand and brief case in the other. If she's not talking on her phone, she is firmly gripping a 24-pack of beer with her large paw." Murphy chuckled and went on, "Maybe she would like one of your cute pink glittery evening bags, Ellen!"

"Murph, you're awful. We really don't know her. God knows what her past has been like. Obviously, she did not marry the man of her dreams, have three kids and iron his button-down shirts he wore to work each day."

Both cousins chuckled. Ellen went on. "But as far as describing her getting home from work, you got it, cousin. Then she goes into her house, and I hear her coming out the back patio door. She joins her boyfriend Kelly and his friends who are having a party out there every afternoon, mind you. Then I can hear her confirming each of their statements with a loud 'Yah,' or 'yah, yah, or yaaah.' She's an expert on every topic. That's why I nicknamed her 'Yah-Yah Girl.' Frequently I hear her erupt mid-sentence or mid-yah with thunderous smoker's cough, like a blubbery whale that had drunk the whole Pacific Ocean. Poor thing. You just know she is going to die of lung cancer or some other horrible thing."

"Oh, Cuz, you are so funny. Tell me again why you think they might be making meth or something?"

"Well, a couple of reasons: First, I smell this sweet stuff – somehow I am able to discern it, even with the heavy tobacco and pot smoke that envelopes their whole yard; second, they keep their front door open almost all the time, even when it's snowing! Finally, every now and then, I see a panel truck go down the alley, stop at their back gate and pick up something. You know, they don't have a trash company like all of the rest of us do. So, I really don't know if one of their friends is hauling their trash for them or if they are picking up something else."

"Wow, it's interesting even in winter they keep their door open and a truck picks up something. I know what you mean about the smoke. It is not pleasant to sit on your patio because of it. You have told me several times, you bring Buttercup in the house because you don't think it is healthy for her to breathe the air. All of your reasons sure seem fishy to me. You know, Ellen, speaking of fishy, if you think you can eat something, maybe we could go to lunch like we planned to do before all of this happened today. I'm getting a little famished."

"Well, now that you mention it, I am hungry. Maybe you can drive and I can keep knitting. I have to get a bunch of these made, you know. I don't know who killed that poor man, but we really need to make sure his demise doesn't stop the tour. I don't want his killer or killers to be responsible for us not having it, and we really need to see where we are on all this tour stuff. Let me 'powder my nose' as they would say in the fifties, and I'll be ready to go."

"Great. While you are doing that, I'll call my office. I need to let all of my agents know what happened. I hope they are not too scared now to volunteer as tour guides. I sure hope nothing has come out on the news yet. I want them to get the information from me first. Oh, I best call all of our committee members and sponsors, too, while I am at it."

"That's really a good idea, Murph. We will want to control the communication as much as we can. For now, we could say the police are actively investigating, and we will let them know of any new developments just as soon as we can."

A short time later, Ellen came back to her living room. Murph was still on the phone but seemed to be wrapping up a conversation. She nodded at Ellen. When she hung up, Ellen asked, "Ready?" Murph nodded again and Ellen patted Sweetie Pie on the head and said to her Airedale Terrier, "Buttercup, guard the house." Then she and Murph walked out the front door.

They saw Annie dressed in an old house dress and worn green sweater, walking around her front yard holding a plastic bag. She was knocking off dandelions with her cane and then -- very wobbly -- stooping down to pick them up and putting them in the bag.

When she saw the cousins, she stopped and squeaked in a high voice to Ellen, "Oh dearie, wasn't that just awful what happened in the alley this morning! We've never had a murder in the neighborhood. Maybe we would have had one sooner if I hadn't told the cops about the Mexican drug gang. Their leader is in jail. I don't understand why Mexicans name their sons after our Lord, Jesus. That's the name of the leader, you know."

"I don't know either, Miss Annie. Maybe we can talk later. We are headed to lunch. It's been quite a day already," Ellen said, hurrying down the sidewalk so she wouldn't have to talk more with the old lady.

Opening her door to Murph's sporty red Chevy Malibu, Ellen let out, "Whew! Thank God I got away from that witch! I so wish things were different with me and Annie. I feel so sorry for her. She basically doesn't have any family here. Once in a while, I have seen an older woman park her car and hobble on her cane up Annie's porch stairs. Why they let someone who is so incapacitated drive is beyond me. There is a senior center close by, and I know they pick seniors up in a bus and bring them there. But Annie never goes. Poor Annie, she is so isolated and so boxed in with memories."

Murph closed her door and put on her cat-eye shaped sunglasses, "Yes, it seems like Annie doesn't have much of a life. She's lucky she still has her eyesight. But she hasn't been that kind to you, Ellen, and, dear cousin, she is not your responsibility. Sweetie, I have just the place for us to have a great lunch and maybe there we can find out more about Hector Hernandez. Buckle up. We're going to my old grade school friend's restaurant, Lupita's Mexican Restaurant. Maybe you remember playing "Queen of the

Mountain" with us when you spent the night with me as a kid? She is very connected to the Hispanic community – I wouldn't be surprised if she doesn't already know about Hector's death – and her nephew worked for me."

"Mexican food sounds great, Murph. It will be good to get out of Englewood. Yes, I do remember running up that hill as fast as I could so I could be the queen of the mountain. I had to run really fast because even then you were smaller than me and could run faster. You know, maybe we can start to figure out this murder by you finding out what you can about the victim from Lupita and Javier, and I'll talk with my neighbors to see if they saw anything or suspect who might have killed poor Hector."

Murph turned on the ignition and rolled down the top to her car. Ellen reached for her knitting, but decided not to get it out since the wind would be whipping all around them. Instead, she dug out of her saddlebag Coach purse her tortoise shell sunglasses and put them on. Then remembering her manners, she turned her head and she and Annie waved goodbye.

CHAPTER FOUR
ANNIE
...ONE OF THOSE PLEASANT WARM DAYS THAT BELIED THE STORM BREWING OVER THE MOUNTAINS...

Murph skillfully steered her red Chevy from the curb and headed to the stop sign at Smith Avenue. She then turned left and headed west to Federal Boulevard.

"That Annie is a kick, knocking off dandelion heads with her cane. Clever. I hope I'm able to be that sharp if I live to 90. Ellen, why do you have so many problems with her? I know you even call her – what's that word? I think it means witch in Italian."

"It's *strega*. Yes, it is the word for witch in Italian. All that wild gray hair, her screechy voice, those intense blue eyes, and her forceful manners remind me of a witch. Annie has turned out to be a real pain in the butt for me, Murph. When I had all those contractors at my house, she'd hobble over as they were getting out of their trucks and interrogate them about what they were doing. Then she would tell them her tale of woe about how her husband died of an early age, how she raised her boy and girl, and how her son died of the same cancer as his dad. The men always stood there and listened to her, after all she is an old woman. What were they to do? Sometimes Annie hampered their work by telling them what they could and could not do. Finally, I would warn each guy about her before they came to my house. It was costing me time and money. I should have talked to Annie directly, but I just did not have the heart to call her on her behavior."

Ellen adjusted her glasses because the wind had blown them to one side of her nose. She went on,

"When the City came out to mark the property lines for the permit for the new fence, Annie was out there in her housedress telling them where the property line between our two houses actually was. She adamantly believes the City had changed it from the time she and her late husband bought their house in nineteen fifty-two. She doesn't like it at all I took down the chain link fence along the back and between our houses and had a 6-foot stockade fence put in. She no longer could spend time surveying the alley or snooping who was in my yard. When I first moved in, I thought I would grow cucumbers in the little space by the chain link fence between our houses. I had planned on giving many to Annie. I quickly learned that wouldn't work because she always would be out there wanting to talk, and I would not get to my gardening."

"Well, as a realtor, Ellen, I can tell you people do dispute property lines from time to time. That's why you have title insurance."

"Yep. I know that. I told her daughter Sandy that when she came from California to visit her mom shortly before Christmas last year. Her daughter told me Annie fell in the alley dumping trash and broke her hip a couple of years ago. That's why she walks with a cane. She refuses to use a walker."

Murph stopped the car at a red light and said, "That attitude probably makes her strong, Ellen. I sure hope you and I never have to use a walker." The light turned green, and Murph accelerated the car.

Ellen's whole body lurched forward. "God, Murph, we're no longer 17-years-old dragging Sixteenth Street, you know! Well, back to Annie. Actually, I would love to help Annie with her garden. Yellow mums, shasta daisies, little pink roses, and irises bloom gaily along the side of her house next to mine. It's proof of her love for flowers and gardening skills of days-gone-by. It desperately needs to be thinned, trimmed, weeded and fertilized, but I don't want to get tangled up in the web of Annie's dependence. It seems to me she needs help, Murph, and Sandy is not doing much about that."

"What does she do about housekeeping and her yard?" Murph yelled above the wind coming into the convertible.

"On Thursdays, a woman from her church comes for four or five hours to do light housekeeping, wash and to take Annie grocery shopping. Obviously, washing windows is not one of her duties, because Annie's windows are filthy. Her side kitchen window looks directly onto my office window. The window sill is lined with small colored bottles. The stained, dirty café curtains have long ago been bleached out by the sun. In a funny way, both Annie's and Kelly's kitchen windows are similar: dirty and lined with bottles." Ellen laughed. The man who cuts her grass, Roland, told me he has known Annie since grade school, but I never see him talking with her."

Stopping at the next stop light, Murph said, "Oh that is sad."

"It sure is, Murph. What she told me about her son is even sadder. One Tuesday before the new fence was built between our yards, Annie had just returned to her yard after carefully wheeling out her small blue trash can to the alley. She saw me in the yard and shrieked my name. I came over to the fence, and she told me, tears welling in her eyes, 'My Johnny was so wonderful. He had a PhD. Those good looking young men who live behind me are the about the same age he was when he died. They are such bums – no education. Brent, who lives right behind me, has been married more than once. For shame – he does have some cute little girls from wife No.2. I used to see that son of his from wife No.1 in the garage with his dad after he came home from work. Brent leaves for work shortly after Sam and his family leave for their paper route. I don't know what Brent does for a living. Axle, the tree guy – why, young women are there all the time. The little girl, who lives there, looks like him – long black hair, big black eyes. He did offer to chop down those branches you keep telling me to take care of so they don't pull down the power line between our houses. Roland will take care of them one of these days. Wish these people would just mind their own business. But, I should be kinder; after all I am a Christian woman!'"

"Wow, Ellen, seeing those men must be tough for her. You mentioned her daughter coming at Christmas time, does her son's family – if he had one – ever see her?"

"Not to my knowledge. The Saturday before Christmas I was sitting on my porch in one of the little iron red chairs next to the matching table. It was one of those pleasant warm days in Englewood that belied the storm which was brewing just over the mountains. There was the rental car parked in front of Annie's house, her daughter from California was visiting and had just come out of her mother's house. Before I could escape to the inside of my house, Sandy strode into my yard and said, 'Mind if I join you? It's such a lovely day.' I got up, walked to the edge of the porch and greeted her. She has lots of blond curly hair and large blue eyes. She looks like an almost exact younger replica of Annie. She climbed the two steps to the porch and sat on the other little red chair. Undoubtedly, the blond is from a bottle, I thought, since Sandy was probably 10 to 15 years younger than me."

Murph took a quick look at Ellen and chuckled. "Me and you, kiddo, don't know anything about those kind of bottles."

Ellen grinned and continued her story. "She said to me 'Hello, I'm Annie's daughter, Sandy. My mother is quite a woman! Before I was born, she was an executive secretary at Gates Rubber Company, which was internationally known for their automobile belts and hoses, and my dad was an electrician with the decades old Bradford Electric. I remember them telling me when I was a little girl that they had met shortly after the war ended at the Trocadero Ballroom at world-famous Elitch Gardens in North Denver.'"

Murph had stopped her car at another red light. "Boy, Ellen, I remember my mom and dad talking about the Trocadero Ballroom. I was there once. Didn't you go, too? Remember, Elitches stayed open all night for high school graduation and had rock bands in the Trocadero?"

"Oh, Murph, I sure do. I remember riding the Wild Cat roller coaster six times that night. I recall the Moonrackers were playing in the Trocadero, and I danced for hours. It was such fun. Oh, and the beautiful flowers in the gardens. Tearing down the beautiful amusement park with its lovely ballroom, was such a loss to Denver. Thank goodness they kept some of the land for a little park. I don't know how many houses they built in the area where the amusement rides were located."

The light turned green, and Ellen continued the story about Annie. "Well, back to what Sandy told me on my porch, she said, 'My dad told me, your mom just glided in with a bunch of giggling girls, wearing a heavenly blue dress, with lots of petticoats. I was smitten, with her blond hair and those sexy blue bedroom eyes. Jimmy Dorsey's band was playing 'Tangerine'. When that good looking, dark-haired Jimmy Dorsey started singing, I rushed over to her, grabbed her hand and started dancing. It was such a magical night.' Sandy continued, 'Shortly after meeting, they married and moved into this brand-new neighborhood. I was born soon after, and my brother came along a couple of years later. Our dad died of a rare cancer when I was eight. My mom is very smart and has helped this neighborhood so much. Why, she spotted a couple of drug deals going down in the alley and had the sense to call the police. They nabbed them. She witnesses stuff going on in the neighborhood all the time.'"

A car full of teenage boys pulled alongside Murph's convertible, "Hi, ladies. You sure look hot in that sexy vehicle." They started giggling and hooting. The driver gunned the car, and it sped off.

Chuckling, Ellen said, "Geez, Murph, after all these years, the boys still like us! Well, back to my conversation with Sandy on the porch, I said that's interesting your mom helps this neighborhood so, but I must tell you, I do not appreciate her coming over and disrupting the workers I have had at this house. It is certainly not okay for her to feed treats to my dog, either."

Sandy interrupted me and said, "Oh, yes. She always fed the dog who lived here before and you know how elusive the city is changing property lines. Mom was real disappointed about your new fence. Hard for her to watch the alley now, you know. She made a deal with the Dells, the people who built your house when they built that big garage. The 3-foot piece of chain link fence you took out next to her yard over to the edge of your garage was really her fence and her property."

"Oh, now I understand why she was screaming so much the day we took down that piece of fence. Sorry, Sandy, all of this should have been handled with the Dells. I have a free and clear title to this house and title insurance. Your mom knew I was putting up a fence. Did she not tell you? If she did, it is strange you did not explain to her about title insurance. If it was really a big deal to her, maybe you could have even looked into some legal recourse if there is any after all these years. Your mom is always so excited when she knows you are coming. Do you stay in touch with her in between your visits? Also, your mom told me your daughter goes to school in Boulder at my alma mater, the University of Colorado. Boulder is like two hours from here. I never see your daughter. I think it would be a big help to your mom if you ladies paid more attention to her. I can only imagine how anxious she was when she saw me take out that fence and all of the other improvements I have made to this house.

You can leave me your contact information if you like. I will let you know of any other changes I make and ask you to communicate them to your mom. I'm sure that would help her, and it would help me immensely if she minded her own business."

Murph slowed down her Chevy and made a right turn off Federal. She was getting close to the restaurant.

Ellen concluded her story about Sandy. "She did give me her contact info. Maybe I should email her and let her know about what happened this morning. I would imagine Annie is a little apprehensive about a murder next door to her. I can tell you, Murph, the night after Sandy left, Mother Nature dumped a foot of snow on us and the temperature plummeted to below zero. Sandy and her car were nowhere in sight. Ninety-four-year-old Annie was alone in her house like she had been for many years."

Murph had been listening to Ellen while she was driving down Federal Boulevard for most of the time. This street had always served as a boundary, separating the Hispanic community from the Caucasian community. There were all sorts of strip centers on it and rundown apartment buildings, probably built in the early eighties when Denver had one of its oil booms. When she turned on Alameda, she ventured through one street after another, including Knox Court, where she used to live as a young girl with her family. They moved to a brand new blond brick house in one of Denver's new suburbs when she was 10. Some of the earliest homes built after WWII were on Knox Court and several surrounding streets. They were small ranch homes covered in square-shaped siding.

Ellen thought, I remember Murph's family had a white one with a red roof. My Aunt Kay had a lovely rock garden and lots of 4 o'clock bushes. But now, many of the yards are dirt, and there are rusted tricycles here and there. But look at that one, every now and then I see a house that has been recently painted and is well taken care of. Yep, I see signs of coming gentrification. This area is great for folks who work downtown since it is close by and has small fairly well-built mid-century homes in a diverse neighborhood. If you lived here and worked there, you would sure have a short commute by car, bus, bike or light rail. I bet many of the new residents are in their twenties.

Murph then took a right into the parking lot by Lupita's. She parked her clean sexy red car in the rundown shopping center. It stood out like a sore thumb. Turning off the ignition, she looked at her cousin and said, "Wow. Poor Annie."

CHAPTER FIVE
HECTOR
... *HE PUT HIS DESIRES AND DREAMS ASIDE*
...

Lupita saw them and opened the door with a big grin on her face. "Murph, oh, excuse me, I should probably call you Mary now since we are all grown up. It's so good to see my special red-haired friend," she said.

"Oh, Lupita, you are the most beautiful 'Queen of the Mountain'!" Murph howled, and the two grown women embraced each other.

"Lupita, do you remember my cousin Ellen, who used to try so hard to keep up with us playing Queen of the Mountain?"

"Oh, my, don't tell me this is the skinny tall kid with the pale red braids! Really?"

"The one and only, and here we are some 65 years later and none of us have scabs and band aides on our knees and elbows," Murph hooted.

"Well, maybe just a little arthritis," Ellen said, grinning and offering Lupita a hug.

"What brings you ladies to Lupita's fine Mexican Restaurant?" Lupita asked, showing them to a booth in the corner.

Murph quipped, "Me and Cuz here are planning a stupendous event and needed a little inspiration. We were in the vicinity, and I thought there's nothing like fine Mexican food to give you a little stimulation." Ellen thought, with a little smirk which looked like an agreeable smile, actually, Lupita, she means indigestion.

"Well, you ladies take a look at the menu. After I get you your food, and you have had a chance to talk about your event, I'll sit down and join you. It is close to closing time after all."

The food arrived about 1:30 and when they were done eating, close to 2, most of the other people had left the restaurant. Lupita came over with a plate of sopapillas, cups, and a pot of freshly brewed decaf coffee.

"You two have stayed in touch all of these years?" Ellen asked.

"Well, we did lose touch after Murph left the 'hood," Lupita said.

"One day, my nephew Javier told me he was going to go to work for a crazy lady who owned her own real estate company named Mary Mahoney. I asked him why she was crazy and he said, 'Well, first she hired me, a Hispanic kid who had just passed his real estate exam; secondly, she has this bright red hair and laughs a lot; and her family and friends call her Murph.' Wow, I said, that sounds like my old friend I went to school with. I do see for sale signs with Mahoney on them. Why don't you ask her where she went to grade school? He did. Murph and Javier came in one day, and we've been friends every since. Your cousin helped him a lot, Ellen."

After pouring herself a cup of coffee, Lupita asked, "So, what's this event you are planning?"

Murph took a drink of her own coffee and replied, "It's our Pink Blossoms Garden and Neighborhood Tour in honor of Mamie Eisenhower. People can either take the tour themselves with a brochure we provide or join one of our tour groups. An architect or other knowledgeable person, like a realtor from my office, or a garden expert will shepherd them around the neighborhood."

Ellen went on, "These 1950s homes – called mid-century modern – are really hot stuff now because they were solidly built and still somewhat affordable.

Both Murph's parents and my parents bought one of these ranch-style homes back then. So many of them were built as a result of the explosion of the Denver area's post WWII population. Of course, we know how popular then First-Lady Mamie Eisenhower from Denver was. She loved the color pink – remember all those crazy pink Christmas ornaments and people dying their poodles pink!"

The three old friends hooted. Murph said, "Yah, my mom even made me a felt poodle skirt!"

Ellen said, "My mom did too, and in neighborhoods like mine where I live today and where the tour will be, there are still thousands of crabapple trees that were planted because Mamie loved their beautiful pink spring blossoms when they didn't get frozen out by one of our late snowstorms. They are truly incredible to see! Murph and I dreamed up this tour in hopes of staving off developers from bulldozing these homes, and then constructing large ugly multi-family complexes on their lots. When people become aware of the history, public outcry and historic preservation efforts increase. It's a great way of promoting Murph's company, and we will donate funds raised to local schools."

"That sounds wonderful," Lupita said. "Where is your neighborhood?"

"Olde Englewood."

Lupita's eyes filled with tears, and she said to Murph, "Is that why you came to my restaurant today Mary Mahoney? One of my former employees was found dead there today, brutally murdered in some alley."

Murph put her hand on Lupita's and said, "Yes. It happened early this morning by Ellen's garage. She is the one who found him."

35

Tears came to Ellen's eyes and she shook slightly, remembering the gory sight she saw this morn.

Waiting a moment for her cousin to gain her composure and hopefully, for Lupita's anger to go away, Murph went on, "The police were all over the alley and neighborhood. But, Lupita, you know – better than most – about how slow police investigations can be, especially when the victim is Hispanic. Ellen and I are doing what we can to try and find the murderer before the tour. People are worried. Apparently, he worked for the guy who lives behind Ellen. The guy has a tree trimming business. He was the one who identified the poor man as Hector Hernandez. Yes, Lupita, that is why I brought Ellen here for lunch. I knew if anyone could help us, it would be you."

Murph didn't even get all her words out before Lupita said sadly and near tears, "Oh, no! He was such a nice kid. Took good care of his mom."

Ellen was crying, too. When she gained her composer she said, "I'm so sorry, Lupita. Someone killed him right behind my house early this morn. I found him when I opened my garage door. Who would kill him? We have a peaceful neighborhood, except for some drug activity from time to time. What can you tell us about Hector? I know people who work for the tree company owner, Axle Kutz, work very hard."

Lupita looked down at her cup, took a slow drink and then replied, "Nice kid. Worked here with his mother. Worked here for a while after her death. He left a couple of years ago. He had been taking some bookkeeping classes and told me he got a bookkeeping job. Unlike most Hispanic young men, he put his desires and dreams aside to start a family young, and instead really worked to get an education. I was happy for him. Restaurant work is hard. We don't get annual increases like they do in the corporate world. Our customers aren't well off, so tips are what they are. I don't know what happened to his bookkeeping job. I did learn this morn he had been murdered in Englewood, and he had recently taken a job with a trash company and was doing some work for a tree trimmer on one of his days off. I understand his body was brutally mutilated."

She stared out a window for a while and then went on, "His dad and brother are in jail. I don't know about any other family. His mom was a very devout Catholic. Maybe Father Louie at Our Lady might know something. I'm so sorry his life ended that way. He was such a good guy."

Sighing deeply, Lupita dabbed at her eyes with a handkerchief she had in her pocket before going on. "His grandparents – if they are still alive - are in Mexico. His mom and dad crossed the border as young teenagers and stayed in Texas for four or five years, each of which his mom had had another child. They were cold and hungry and his dad spent what little money they had on tequila and drugs. He gambled, too. Because of his gambling debts, Hector and his family fled to Colorado. For awhile, Hector's parents worked in the fields in the San Luis Valley. His dad eventually found a job in a coal mine. One day there was an altercation outside of the mine and Hector's dad was thrown in the slammer on suspicion of murder. The cops determined he did not kill the man, but was an accessory. He spent three years in jail."

Reaching for the coffee pot, Lupita poured herself another cup before continuing. "Somehow Hector's mom Maria, who was such a hard worker, kept the family together with neighbors and the church helping out. When Hector's dad got out, the family moved to Denver. His mom started working here and his dad got a day labor job. Maria became pregnant again. Hector's dad had another fight at work and this time he was not only thrown in jail, but was sentenced for 10-15 years. Hector and his older brother dropped out of high school and began working to support the family. Besides, they really struggled in school; none of them could read very well. Hector's older brother got in trouble with the law, too. He ended up in juvenile jail. Hector knew he needed more lucrative work than what he was doing working in the same restaurant as his mom. He went back and got his GED. Hector's mom was my worker, but more importantly, she was my friend." Lupita put her face in her hands and wept.

The three women all sat in the booth. Ellen starting crying again. Finally Murph said, "Thank you, Lupita. We are so sorry." She patted Marie's hand then said, "We'll keep you up on our progress." She and Ellen quietly left the restaurant after putting down money for their lunch and a sizeable tip.

The cousins got back in the hot red Chevy.

In silence, they drove through the nearby Projects, government paid housing also built shortly after WWII, and reflected on this shadow side of Denver. The Projects were ugly. Windows were broken, the grass long gone. Run-down rusted cars everywhere. It was very depressing. How did anyone get out of this environment legally? Both women, having lived in the metro area all of their lives, had an understanding of drugs, drug dealing and prostitution as a means for supporting yourself and your family in this god-awful area.

Before the cousins were born in 1946 and 1947, shortly after the end of World War II, this area of town for decades had been associated with Mexican gangs. There was no hope here. Many dads were in jail or dead and their wives or lovers strapped with kids they had a hard time feeding, clothing and keeping warm. The girls seemed to have an easier time than the boys, who seemed to be driven to gangs as a way life. These organizations protected the neighborhoods and forged some ethnic pride.

The cops were not trusted and did not seem to offer any security. Further, brutality by the police was a way of life here or so it seemed. Society and the cops didn't accept them, but the gangs did. Members were known to carry knives and to know how to use them. Staying in school beyond the 8th grade was rare. Many families attended the Catholic Church, but the church was ineffective in solving the problems these families and boys faced. Furthermore, sex was a way of proving manhood, and sex and birth control were condemned by the church. As soon as a girl got pregnant, she dropped out of school and the road to poverty got wider. Stealing cars and merchandize was common. Eventually, the gangs got into drugs, especially marijuana, which was so common in Mexico and easy to get across the border.

Once they drove out of the Projects area, Murph exclaimed, "The fact Hector was still alive in his mid-30s was amazing. Actually, even more astounding, is Javier's success. Lupita's nephew sure has a prosperous real estate office located in this area. Javier works so hard. He actively promoted this part of town and works closely with the city council to improve streets, trash removal and pavement of alleys. I think they realize that because of him the tax base is going up in this area and the city services are not such a financial drain as they have been for years. Then, the people who work for Javier volunteer in the many civic activities he sponsors. Several Hispanic reporters Javier knows work for the local paper and television stations. He is very adept at getting information to them which wound up on the news. As a result, people began considering the area as desirable, especially first-time homeowners, who could only qualify for low monthly payments. I can hardly wait to introduce him and his workers to you, Ellen. They volunteered to be tour guides at our event.

Murph pulled up to Ellen's home. "I'll call you in the morn, hon. I'm going to catch up with Javier. It seems so strange Hector studied bookkeeping, but was in your alley working for a trash company and Axle, too. Try and get some sleep. If you get spooked, don't hesitate to call me. You have been through a lot today, dear lady."

Ellen went in her house and hugged Buttercup and put her cat in her lap. She got up, made herself a cup of cocoa and then sat in her old rocker and rocked and cried.

CHAPTER SIX
A FUNNY ALLEY
...HOW DARE A WOMAN STAND UP TO HIM AND NOT DO WHAT SHE WAS TOLD...

Sipping her coffee and responding to an email from a tour committee member, Ellen's phone rang.

"Hello, Ms. Lane. This is Officer Green. I am planning on stopping by this morning to ask you a few more questions."

"Oh, sure, Officer. Could you give me an hour or so? I am answering emails from our committee members who are concerned about the tour and about me, too, I might add. And, please call me Ellen."

An hour later Officer Dan Green showed up on Ellen's porch. Buttercup started barking and Sweetie Pie ran and hid under the couch.

Putting Buttercup in a stay, Ellen opened the door. "Please come in, Officer Green."

"Good morning, Ellen. I don't have a lot of questions."

"Would you like to sit at my dining room table or the kitchen one?"

"The kitchen would be great."

"Coffee, Officer, and another piece of fudge?"

"Thanks, Ellen, both would be appreciated."

"Officer, before we get started, I don't know how much you can tell me about your investigation; but, I can tell you my tour committee is very anxious because a killer might be loose in this neighborhood. Our ticket sales are way down, and we have had sponsors calling us wondering if the tour will go on. What can you tell me, so far?"

"We are actively pursuing the investigation

Ellen. You are right, as a police officer, I can tell you very little about the specifics of the murder. From my experience, this doesn't seem like a random killing, so I don't think people unrelated to the murderer need to worry. We are in the process of interviewing all suspects and reviewing the forensics. You could tell people that. This does take time, unfortunately. Now, Ellen, I do have one question about your dog and then I would like you to tell me why you put up a thick yellow chain across your driveway Tuesday night."

"What about my dog? Buttercup is wonderful!"

"Well, I was wondering if Buttercup woke you up barking or started barking when you let her out in the morning?"

"Mmmm. Buttercup is not one of those dogs who bark at fireworks or thunder. She barks if someone comes to the door. The only time she barks in the back yard is when someone is walking their dog down the alley. She doesn't even bark at all the commotion in the alley when Axle's people come to work. Yesterday morning was very typical how we start our day. My alarm went off, and I jumped out of bed, and Buttercup got up from her bed on the floor next to mine. I let her out and then fed her. I don't remember her barking after I let her outside."

"I see, Ellen. Buttercup is very different than my beagle Baxter who barks at everything! Please fill me in on why you string the yellow chain across your driveway."

Putting her index finger under her nose and gently rubbing it across her upper lip, Ellen said, "Boy, Officer, you would think it would be an easy question to answer, but actually it's a lot to relay. Let's see: first, there was the 'watering hole,' then the great adventure with PU Trash Services, and finally, Axle's threats and all his vehicles! I tried so hard to work with Axle and

PU Services and finally, I had to get the City involved. That's why I have had so much email contact with Mark McCoy."

After taking a sip of her coffee, Ellen continued. "Officer Green, it has not been easy living in this neighborhood. This alley has been a huge challenge for me. First, I was worried about my safety because there was just a chain link fence in the back, with a gate, no less. The funny little cement alley off the street east of Emerald dead ends at the dirt alley behind my house. So anyone could walk or drive down the cement alley, open the gate and come into my yard, steal my nice patio furniture, break into the house or god-knows-what! So I had a big stockade fence installed along the back of my yard, and between my yard and my neighbor's on the north, Annie's yard. Fortunately, my neighbor on the south, Kelly, already had put up a stockade fence in front of the chain link which originally separated our two homes. His wood fence protected my yard from people hopping over the fence from the alley and gave me a place on the original metal fence where I could attach my chain with a lock. I am able to secure the chain on the north side of my garage by attaching it to a large eye hook, which I screwed through a piece of wood that had been added years ago to protect the garage from vehicles missing the turn and running into it. Also, I bought one of those super expensive security screen doors to cover my back door on the patio."

Green stated, "Oh, I can see why you would want a big wood fence all around your yard for security, Ellen. Since the alley is narrow, I comprehend why your driveway goes from the north to the south, instead of straight back to the alley. But, what I don't understand is why you stretch a big thick yellow chain across your driveway. "

"I have to put up with all those trash trucks Englewood allows to operate here. Do you know I counted at least eleven trash companies? Some of them have such humorous names. Off the top of my head I can name: Pack Man, Garbage Man, the giant PU Services, and Best Junk."

Confirming Ellen's statement, Green said, "Yep, it is interesting we have so many in Englewood. I guess the city wants to be fair to all businesses. But eleven or more? Crazy!"

"Officer, you're right. It is crazy. So, every Wednesday those companies, who have customers on Emerald and Olive Streets, barrel down the small cement alley which intercepts the narrow dirt alley. I guess the cement alley was put in so there could be two exists to the alley since the pretty two old farm houses north of my house face Smith Avenue and were there long before the town existed. One of those houses, if not both of them, would have had to be demolished for a regular alley with a north and south exit to be put in."

"Yes, I agree, Ellen. It is a strange alley configuration, but your reasoning about the farm houses being there before it was built makes sense."

"You know Officer Green, I don't know why the little alley off Olive Street is paved, and the alley running behind our houses isn't. I do know the people who built this house, and Annie and Sam got together and paid for the dirt alley to be paved immediately behind our houses. I am glad they did. Dirt is so dirty," Ellen giggled before going on. "Last summer I first contacted McCoy when I got the brush off from his department about what I call 'the watering hole' in the alley. You see, as a result of the tight turn trash trucks have to make to go down from the cement alley to the dirt alley, they carve out a large deep hole near the edge

44

of my driveway where the paving, which the homeowners paid for, ends. This hole is almost always filled with water, which comes from melting snow or rain. It rarely completely evaporates, even during last summer's days of over a hundred degrees. It reeks."

Ellen took another sip of her coffee. Buttercup went to the back door, and Ellen let her out before continuing, "Early last summer when I was bringing my trash can to the edge of the alley, I saw Axle in the alley. He smiled at me. He was pleasant to me then. I must say I did suspect he secretly despised me, and saw me as a boney, nervous looking older woman. He probably was jealous because I obviously had money enough to put up this big wood fence and make a number of improvements to this house. That summer day when we were both in the alley I was in a feisty mood and told him I hated this goddamn watering hole. I didn't understand why people have not complained to the city, and I sure didn't understand why the city allowed all these trash trucks in here."

Green asked, "What did Axle say?"

"He said, 'You said it, Ma'am,' and batted his big brown eyes while slightly twitching the large muscles in his arm. He went on, 'I'm going to get some gravel and dump it in this hole!' You know, I think he thinks he is quite the ladies' man. A couple of days later, he filled up the hole. Unfortunately, our neighbor Sam saw him and called the City Zoning Control department. He and Sam are not on the best of terms because Axle blocks access to the alley when Sam and his wife are returning from their early morning paper route and because of all of Axle's extra cars parked in Brent's driveway, which is directly behind their garage. McCoy's old department drove down the alley and gave Axle a ticket for hampering with city property! Axle was fuming."

Ellen leaned back in her chair and laughed. "The next time I saw Axle in the alley, he told me all about it. 'The blond-haired wimp, why doesn't he mind his own business? He's always yelling at me and my workers. He tries to get past us to get to his garage just as we are going to work. What does he care if I rent some space from my next door neighbor Brent to park a few cars I am working on for my side business? I work very hard, after all. The rent money helps Brent with the legal expenses of his kid's fatal car accident, which killed him and everyone in his car.' After that conversation with Axle, I had had enough with this watering hole. So I emailed the zoning enforcement department."

Standing up, Ellen asked Green if he wanted more coffee or fudge. After filling his cup and getting him another piece of fudge, Ellen excused herself to use the bathroom.

When she returned, Green said, "What did McCoy do?"

"McCoy responded he would get the engineering department to assess the situation because he told me, 'The City cannot have private citizens do the repairs since the risk is tremendous. City budgets are really tight. I will see what I can do.' About two weeks later, I spotted a city engineering crew of three in the alley. They walked around the hole, kicked at the dirt, looked down and up the alley, and then drove off. It took about fifteen minutes for them to do their assessment. McCoy then emailed me back and said the City would be filling the hole."

Ellen took a deep breath, gazed at her crabapple outside the window over her sink and then continued, "A large City of Englewood dump truck a week later did come lumbering down the small alley and parked directly in front of my driveway. Four men hopped out as I gawked from my back kitchen window. The truck poured a bunch of small rocks in the hole and a couple of the men got out rakes and leveled them. The solution lasted only several months because the big trash trucks skidded through it each Wednesday, hurling the rocks all across the alley and my driveway. Soon the watering hole was full again of water and all sorts of debris, much to my aggravation. And yesterday, the hole was filled with the victim's blood. When this is over, the City had better fill that hole with cement. Actually, I think they should pave this whole alley."

Green stared at Ellen and then said, "I can see why you are so angry." He had been taking notes during their whole conversation. After writing in his notebook for several more minutes, he stood up and asked Ellen if he could use her bathroom.

When Green returned, Ellen went on and told him about the yellow chain, her solution to the trials with PU Services' trucks using her driveway to make the turn down the alley. She told him how she had contacted their customer service department, and they told her they would speak to the drivers.

"But to no avail, Officer Green. So one day I placed my trash can at the edge of the driveway right in the middle and flanked it with pots and plastic waste baskets so they could not drive forward. I came home and found my trash dumped all over my driveway and my pots and baskets strewn. I saw Axle in the alley several days later. He told me PU Services just stopped their truck and threw all of my stuff and then drove on my driveway to make the turn in the alley. He said, 'I stay home on Wednesdays and do paperwork. I saw these guys out there and went out there to tell them to knock it off.'"

Ellen cleared her throat and went on, "I told Axle I appreciated him doing this because I know my cement is not thick enough to continually be pounded by the weight of their truck. They are so arrogant! Such a large company, national in scope. Residential pick-up is just frosting on the cake. I must say I was delighted Axle would care enough to help me. He can be so charming, you know. I decided the solution would be to string up a strong, thick, very visible yellow chain. I purchased one and two locks from Home Depot. Each Tuesday night I hang the chain about 3-feet high from my garage to the chain link fence which borders my property with my neighbor Kelly's. I put the PU Services trash can on the outside of the chain, just on the edge of my driveway. This allows them to pick up the trash, but does not give them access to the driveway."

She got up. Went to her back door and let Buttercup back inside. The Airedale went up to Officer Green and sniffed his legs. Ellen sat back down and told Buttercup, "Settle." The dog went under the table and laid down by her owner's feet.

"Now, about Axle and his vehicles and his threats," Ellen told the cop. "Each morning Axle's workers start arriving to his house about seven and dawdle in the alley until Axle tells them what to do. The workers wear their green Axle's Tree Service t-shirts, just like the poor man who was murdered. I rarely see the same face twice. A few women mix in with the men from time to time. The workers park their dilapidated vehicles on the street or seem to come from nowhere. I'm assuming they must be day laborers Axle picks up, or they take the Broadway bus to Smith Avenue and then they walk to his house."

Green turned the page in his notebook and Ellen saw him write the word Axle at the top of the page before continuing, "The loitering workers are frustrating, especially when I need to get to my 8 a.m. yoga class Wednesday mornings. They fill up the alley. If I don't get out by 7:15, traversing the alley becomes a real problem as workers back up trucks from Axle' s garage and side yard and load them with equipment. Of course, Wednesday mornings are far worse because the various trash trucks invariably almost careen into the workers, trucks and equipment as they turn into the alley. They blast their horns. Axle comes out and tries to appease them. One Wednesday, I backed out of my driveway, late for yoga class, and cussed and glared at Axle. Get your equipment and workers out of here. You have no right to block this public alley, I yelled at him. Axle screamed back at me 'Just go down the dirt alley instead of trying to drive up the cement alley.'"

Green wrote faster and faster, trying to keep up with Ellen's story. He got to the end of the page and quickly turned it, just in time to hear her response to Axle.

"I retorted, I am not going down the dirt alley. I don't have time today, and I have a right to use this public cement alley, and not have to take my time going out of my way to accommodate you. Axle came to my car with a threatening look and arms raised. I'm calling the cops, I told him. I did and also snapped a bunch of photos with my phone. Axle was enraged. I worried he might hit me. I'm sure he was thinking how dare a woman stand up to him and not do what she was told. I think he feared the cops would see what a mess he made of the alley. He yelled back, 'You are trying to drive me away from my home and ruin my small business.' He huffed up the hill and ordered his workers to back the trucks out of the alley so I could pass. I was shaking with anger. Once I got out of the alley, I emailed the photos to McCoy. The city issued Axle a warning letter about vehicle violations both on private (parking on the grass on the side of his house) and public right-of-way (alley). The cops also visited with him about his vehicles." Pausing, Ellen helped herself to a piece of fudge and slowly ate it. Putting her index finger across her nose, the rest of her fingers and nose covered her mouth and chin. Smirking inside, Ellen realized she would be meeting with Axle's landlady, Barbara Evans, also known as BB, in a couple of hours. She also had to be a woman who dared to stand up to him and not do what she was told.

Officer Green looked softly at the small gray haired woman and thought she had a lot of courage and guts. If Axle was the killer, he could understand why he draped the body over the yellow chain. Green glanced through each page of his notes and said, "Thank you, Ellen, for all of this information. I'll keep you informed as much as I can about our progress." He then scooted his chair from the table. Both Buttercup and Ellen stood up and walked him to the door.

CHAPTER 7
AXLE
... EVEN THIS TOUGH OL' BROAD NEEDS A LITTLE LOVE OR MAYBE THE ILLUSION OF LOVE ...

Ellen sat on her bed looking into her closet, thinking about her meeting with Barbara Evans, owner of Denver's famous strip club, The Teasing Tigress, and pondering what to wear to the appointment, scheduled shortly after the establishment closed at 2 p.m. *What should I wear to a strip joint?* My God, what have I gotten myself into? I've driven past this place a zillion times in my life and never ever thought I would go there. Let's see. I have seen a few women in business suits go in the door at lunch time with other men and women. I know. I'll wear a pair of black pants and a simple sweater. After all, I am not a customer, but a member of the tour committee trying to get a donation. I doubt anyone has brought her a plate of fudge. Ha ha.

Promptly at two, Ellen turned her silver Honda CRV into the parking lot of the Teasing Tigress, located at the corner of Mississippi Avenue and Santa Fe Drive. The long low metallic blue building, with a vivid graphic of a large pouncing tigress covering at least half of it had been there for all of Ellen's life. What had changed was the number of lanes on both streets. They each sported six. When she was a girl, Santa Fe and Mississippi were both two-lane streets. Her father frequently drove their family car down it since the new interstate highway, I25 was being constructed. To get to downtown to her dad's company, located in the now old warehouse district, they either took Broadway, which had lots of stop signs and even stop lights, or

Santa Fe, which was part of US Highway 85. Her mom didn't start driving until Ellen was 10 years old.

After she parked her car, she heard a big burly guy telling a man in a rundown Dodge gray sedan, "Hey fella, we're closed now and don't open until four. Why don't you come back then?"

"Screw you," the man said and gunned his car out of the parking lot unto Mississippi Avenue.

Coming over to Ellen's car, the burly man said, "Sorry about his language. Ms. Evans asked me to wait for you and escort you into her office. We close at two, after the lunch crowd leaves and reopen at four."

He opened her car door, and Ellen slowly got out, carefully holding the plate of fudge in one hand. Ellen thought, I wish I could just hop out like I used to be able to. Now I have to slowly get out or my back hurts too much. I'd offer him a piece – but Ellen you can't say that -- he might take it the wrong way. A little smile flickered across the gray-haired woman's face as she thought of the humorous word connection as she walked up to the door with the burly man.

He led Ellen to Barbara's office. When Ellen walked in, she realized the walls were all one-way mirrors, and thought Barbara keeps her eye on things!

"Hello, Ms. Lane. I am Barbara Evans."

"Nice to meet you, Ms. Evans."

The women stood facing each other for a brief minute, each summing up the other woman.

Barbara Evans thought, well, I'll be. This is not what I expected. From her saucy hair cut, natural gray hair and mostly her eyes which seem to look into the soul, Ellen Lane looks to have been around the block in life and can probably hold her own. I bet she and Axle have had a tussle or two.

Facing Barbara, Ellen surmised, this is the woman I saw in Axle's yard. Yep. She sure does have big breasts. I don't think they are real. What a great nickname for her. I bet she is pushing 60. Had no idea what she would wear to work. Actually, she looks very professional in her tweed pants, silk sweater, and black jacket. Her subdued floral scarf is lovely. She has to be a real judge of character or she would not be in this business, for sure.

"Please have a seat, Ms. Lane, and feel free to call me BB. Everyone does."

"Thank you, BB, and please call me Ellen."

Ellen sat down in one of the two wingback chairs, which was upholstered in a gold embossed fabric and faced BB's desk. She said, "I must say my original purpose for meeting with you is the same; but, the circumstances certainly have changed. I assume you know a man was found in my driveway brutally murdered a couple of days ago, and Axle, my neighbor, is believed to be a person of interest since the man was wearing one of his company's green t-shirts and neighbors heard them arguing over pay just the day before."

BB leaned forward and said, "Look Ellen, why don't we talk about why you originally came here. I think you are the first woman from my parents' old neighborhood who ever walked through these doors."

"Okay, first, I brought you this fudge I made, and second, you're right, I have never been in the Teasing Tigress. Although being a Denver native, I have driven by it a million times," Ellen said, handing BB the plate of fudge.

"So, Ellen, thank you for this beautiful candy. I can't remember ever getting a gift like this. Please tell me about it and why you are giving it to me."

"You are welcome, BB. Let me start by telling you about our walking tour of the neighborhood and

53

why we are having a fudge sale that day. The tour's main purpose is to bring awareness to our wonderful mid-century-modern area. We don't want developers coming in and tearing all of our houses down and then building McMansions or those god-awful condominiums on the land. Our Pink Blossoms Garden and Neighborhood Tour committee wanted to contact everyone along our route. We are inviting those homeowners with kids in school to participate in our Mamie's Fudge sale since all the donations will be given to local schools. Also, we wanted to invite any homeowners who have a business to be a sponsor. We did a property search and found out you owned your parent's old house. I did a little more research and found out you are the proprietress of the one-and–only Teasing Tigress, a Denver landmark, for sure!"

"Yes, I agree with you. That neighborhood is great. I do remember something about Mamie being known for her fudge." BB looked at her, twirled a light brown dyed and permed curl above her ear, "And you, Ellen, have the guts to come in here and ask me for a donation. I am impressed."

Ellen responded, "I knew it was useless to ask Axle since he has a hard time paying his workers. I would have liked to invite the woman who lives with him, or did – I am not sure if she still does or not -- to participate in the fudge sale. She has a darling little girl. Axle has caused a lot of angst in the alley, so I thought some participation from you might help the situation. And, frankly, I know Evans Enterprises, Inc., not The Teasing Tigress, is your official business name."

Even though there were no ashtrays on her desk, BB sputtered what sounded to Ellen as a soft smoker's cough, "I am honored to help, Ellen. My parents built that home and lived in it for 60 years. I'll have a check cut for you and mailed first thing in the morning."

"Thank you, BB."

Ellen knew it was time for her to go, but she wanted BB to hear about her trials with Axle. "You know, BB, Axle has a voracious temper, and I believe he is operating his business illegally from your house, probably because he can't afford a building and an equipment yard. I did not want to have shouting matches with him or get the police involved, but I have. Frankly, I am having a hard time believing he killed the man. I think he uses his temper as a weapon, even a bluff, but I don't think he has it in him to kill someone. I was in my car in the garage, waiting for the police to escort me back into my house. My neighbors had gathered in the alley and one of them told me he heard the head cop's remarks. It sounded like Axle had been in jail before. Do you know if this is true, BB? It's bad enough thinking Axle might have killed him, but worse thinking he might have killed someone before." Ellen dropped her head not wanting BB to see how shook up she was. She didn't realize seeing the dead man on the chain had affected her that much. She was near tears and shaking slightly.

BB took a deep breath and said, "About five years ago, I had a car accident. Nothing major, but my car was dinged up. It would have cost me more in insurance premium increases than to just take care of it myself. So, I brought it over to Ray's just off Mississippi and Santa Fe. Ray gave me an estimate that was reasonable and said he had a new guy, Axle, who was really good. He introduced me to him. What can I say? I was immediately bowled over by his looks and great body. Now I recognize I am in the body business, so I keep my personal wants and desires behind a very thick wall, if you will. Well, somehow this guy got through."

Gazing across the room, BB seemed to be considering telling her more. She brought her eyes back to Ellen and said, "Axle fixed my car just fine and somehow we started having 'little meetings' in my bed. It was great, Ellen. Everyone – even this tough ol' broad -- needs a little love or maybe just the illusion of love. I don't know. I found out I was no exception. It didn't last long before I came to my senses and said no more. But I was hooked on helping Axle. Underneath is a very gentle man who has been deeply injured emotionally. When the renters left my late parent's house, I offered it to Axle. Also, I gave him a little investment money for the tree trimming business he wanted to start. He's supposed to pay me back someday, but I have not seen a cent yet. It's okay. The man and his story really touched me. I don't think he is the murderer despite how that guy died and despite that he worked for Axle. You know, Axle takes good care of my parent's old house. I know he is super busy, but when a tree came down in the yard next door and almost took down the fence between the two properties, he and the neighbor worked all of one Sunday to remove that tree. The guy and Axle worked well together. I understand the neighbor does maintenance for Ft. Logan Mental Hospital."

BB took a deep breath, coughed again and then continued, "Yes, I bet Axle was plenty scared when a dead man, who used to work for him, was found in your driveway, Ellen. As far as the past, a long time ago, Axle came home early one day from his dad's auto body shop where he worked. He had just graduated high school and was planning on signing up with the Marines that day. He arrived home and saw his father beating his eight-month-pregnant, 40-something-old-mother. Then, his big brother jumped into the room with a very large butcher knife they used on the farm. He drove the knife into his dad, who was on top of his wife, slugging her. He killed him and, accidently, his mother, since his thrust was so great and the knife was so long. Then, the brother took the knife to himself. Axle was afraid the cops would think he did it since his brother, his dad and his poor mom were dead, so he took off in the family sedan which was faster than the truck he drove. He was picked up almost at the state line. I don't know what he was charged with, but they did throw him in the slammer for stealing the car. It was so unfair."

BB continued, "Axle's dad was a brutal man who believed the best way to keep his wife from having affairs was to keep her pregnant. He beat her on a regular basis as well as all of his children. He was a violent drunk. As he sank lower and lower into alcoholism, he relied more and more on Axle to run his auto body repair shop, which was in the little town near their farm. Axle's brothers and some sisters had the same problem, too. I don't know if any of them are still alive."

Although BB could hardly talk because she was so choked up, she went on. "The story was so unbelievable I had to do some research on it and found it to be true. Axle shouldn't have been thrown in jail, but admitted in a psych hospital for awhile. Maybe that is why your neighbors thought the cop implied this was the second time Axle has been accused of murder. I don't think he could have done it because of what he witnessed in his home, and further the guy doesn't even drink, let alone use drugs."

She and Ellen just sat back in their chairs for a while, deeply breathing and thinking about the horror and the injustice Axle experienced.

"Wow, BB! How awful and how unfair. What about the kids I see at his house every now and then? They look like Axle. What about the woman who lives in the house with him and the little girl?"

"Oh, yes, I am not surprised you see kids with Axle from time to time. After Axle got out of the slammer, he married one of his high school sweethearts. They had two boys. The marriage didn't last. They divorced. The woman in the house with the kid, I think, was a fling Axle had after we broke up. The child is darling. Looks just like him. Her mother is one of those weak type women who can't seem to leave even though I have reason to believe Axle is abusive. I think she worries about supporting herself and the little girl."

"I hate to say it, BB, but her nickname in the neighborhood is 'Ms. Mouse,' and the little girl's name is 'Little Mouse.'"

BB leaned back in her chair and Ellen knew it was time to go. "So, Ellen, how long have you been on your own? You're pretty and skinny. I would think there would be a "Mrs." in front of Lane."

"I've been single a long, long time and have no intention of adding a "Mrs." in front of my name!" Ellen laughed a little.

"I'd be careful, Ms. Lane. Like I said, we all need a little love."

BB stood up and the two women shook hands and said goodbye. Ellen looked out the window before heading out the door to her car. Sure enough there was a line – mostly men, but a few women, waiting to get in when the Teasing Tigress reopened at 4 p.m. She had never understood this perverse business, but BB's words came back to her, "Everyone needs a little love or maybe the illusion of love."

The burly man appeared in the door and

escorted Ellen back to her Honda.

Pulling out of the parking lot, Ellen saw the big black hull of the once flagship operation of Gates Rubber Company and across from it the new condominiums, which had been constructed after the mammoth Samsonite Luggage Company had been demolished. Ellen thought, no wonder the Teasing Tiger has been so popular for so many years. Both of these international manufactures employed thousands of workers. Plus, with all the trains in this area, the strip joint undoubtedly had lots of railroad people, too. When she got to the stop light at Mississippi and Santa Fe, it turned red and Ellen's thoughts drifted back to her conversation with BB. Snorting out loud, Ellen scoffed at BB's caution about adding a Mrs. to her name. Little did Ellen know love would find her soon in her own very strange alley.

CHAPTER 8
SAM
... AND THEN, UNASHAMED, HE WEPT LARGE NOISY TEARS ...

The next morning Ellen was deadheading her yellow daffodils, which she had planted the previous autumn in front of her yellow home, when she spotted Sam doing the same in his yard. Ellen put down her clippers and started walking towards Sam. He was her favorite neighbor. The two of them had spent many hours discussing various plants and gardening methods. She was eager to tell him about her visit with BB and get his take on the gruesome murder in their neighborhood.

As she walked towards Sam, she reminisced about meeting him. God, I remember the day I met Sam. Yep, it was soon after I moved in this house. Shortly before Halloween, we got our first snow. Big saucer-size snowflakes tumbled from the sky and completely covered all of the yellow, fern-like locust leaves on my grass and the sidewalks. The snow was so beautiful, but so yucky, too. I remember trying to find snow boots and a shovel, which wasn't easy since I had just moved into this home. By the time I got all bundled up and looked out the windows again, the sidewalks were shoveled. I cried with glee, a snow angel lives on Emerald Street!

"Hi, Sam. I was just thinking about the day I met you. Remember we had our first snow and you shoveled my walk? I looked out my window and spotted the angel with a big coat and a stocking hat on top of his shoulder-length golden blond hair sliding his shovel from my sidewalk to Annie's. I bounded out the door, trotted after you to thank the angel. I will never forget my amazement when you reached in your pocket and brought out a small slender wooden box, similar to my pencil box I had in the third grade. You held your artificial larynx up to your throat and said, 'No problem. I always do Annie's and I thought I would do yours as well.'"

Sam shrugged his shoulders with a twinkle in his kind blue eyes. He pulled out his voice box and said, "You, Ellen, know how grateful I am to be on this earth. I am so lucky to be here, given my wild crazy lifestyle. He shrugged his shoulder with a sparkle in his blue eyes. I really wasn't home much when Keith was little and Nancy's parents were dying because I was always on the road driving my truck during the day and always partying on the road at night. Yes, I partied hearty!" Sam wiped tears from his eyes. "And I've caused them so much additional pain. I was so sick before the surgery and then through all the chemotherapy and stuff. I was a real obnoxious burden. I just hope I have enough time left to make some amends to them."

"Oh, Sam, you crazy angel," Ellen said, and she gave Sam a hug. He wasn't much bigger than Ellen. At 5-foot, 2-inches and 120 pounds, it was easy for her to embrace him. "You know, Sam, even though there is no emotion reflected in your monochromatic words, I can tell by your face and baby blues you are a humble man who cares for others and tries to help whenever you can."

Pulling the artificial larynx from his pants pocket again, Sam told Ellen, "Had another doc appointment yesterday. Good news. Always tough going to see him because me and my wife know a reoccurrence is probably around the corner. More good news – Keith has a lacrosse game today and a regional meet tomorrow. I just want to live long enough to see him graduate from high school. Axle is a pain, Ellen, but he is just an annoyance, unless he really did kill that poor man." Then, unashamed, Sam wept large noiseless tears.

Ellen thought his guilt was what motivated Sam to live in a house where a thick wall of his wife's cigarette smoke crept into every cranny and darkened all of the windows. God knows Nancy has had enough trouble in her life. Don't judge her, Ellen, for hanging on to the pleasure and release smoking gives her.

"Sam, guess where I was yesterday?"

He looked at her and raised his bushy blond eyebrows.

"The Teasing Tigress! Did you know BB – Axle's landlady – owns The Teasing Tigress?"

Sam nodded his head.

"She's sending us a donation for the tour and told me interesting stuff about Axle."

Sam's eyes lit up. Ellen thought gee, I wonder if Sam was ever a patron of the Teasing Tigress. He sure used to know how to have fun. I remember he told me he partied every night on the road when he was an interstate truck driver. Doesn't anymore. Cancer devastated his life two years ago. The disease took his voice box and his career and the image he held of himself as a cool dude.

Sam said, "Did you talk about the murder? Does she know the cops consider him a person of interest? Surely, she knows about the trouble we have had with Axle."

Ellen responded, "Yes, she knows about the murder and that the cops questioned him. I told her about our trials and tribulations with Axle. But she doesn't think he could murder a person. She told me about some awful, awful things had happened to him as a kid and a teenager. Axle has been through a lot."

"Well, I think he could have murdered the guy. He was in a rage that one day when he got so angry at me. Who knows, Hector could have pulled a knife on him when Axle didn't have the money to pay him. You and I know since we grew up here, the weapon of choice for guys like Hector is a knife. Believe me, they can quickly pull one. Maybe, big Axle somehow knocked it out of his hand, grabbed him and squeezed him or punched him so hard he nearly killed him. The guy was probably unconscious when Axle took the lopper to his neck. You know, Ellen, Axle is mad at you for all of the trouble you have given him. He is not used to females standing up to him. I'm thinking he killed Hector and then threw him over your chain to spite you. The pole up the butt was a real statement. It would take someone very strong to ram it through jeans and shorts and bones."

"Geez, Sam. You really think Axle could have done it? I don't know. Yes, he sure gets angry quickly. Storms around a lot in the alley, screaming when people don't let him have his way."

"If Axle didn't do it, I am thinking it was one of Axle's workers or maybe someone who worked with Hector on the trash truck crew he was on. For those jobs, companies get whoever they can to work for them. Probably one of them knew our alley was used for drug runs and the cops might be too stupid to think of that since the head drug dude is in jail."

"You could be right, Sam. I can't imagine working on a trash truck. Hopping up and down to pick up cans must be very tiring and the smell. Awful!"

"Been thinking about the murder, Ellen, particularly the timing. It must have happened after the time we left around 4 a.m. and when you found him at 7 or so. That's a 3-hour time period when most folks are still sleeping. Cops must have taken Axle's tools for fingerprints. Wonder if he is still a person of interest since he is back home. Did Buttercup bark? I would think she would have, because of the smell of all the blood. Of course, our dogs were in the house because it is too hard for us to take them with us. We often open and close the car doors as we get papers for our customers on our paper route. Keith left for school, thank goodness, after the body was taken down. That would have been a horrible scene for him to see."

"I know what you mean, Sam. I have been thinking about the murder too, and yes, it was a horrible scene to see," Ellen said as tears came to her eyes.

"Don't know how heavy that equipment is, Ellen. I keep thinking it would take a very strong person to ram the tree loppers where he did. You know, the cops have been busy extracting blood out of the watering hole. What an awful job! I wonder what the official cause of death is. All that blood -- you'd think dogs would be constantly barking or foxes and coyotes coming around."

"You know, Sam, I was pretty much in shock that day. Buttercup is not a barker, and I don't remember her barking at all. My cousin came by when the cops were talking with me. When they were called to the alley for something, we decided to go out to lunch like we had planned to before all of this happened. So I was gone a good part of the afternoon."

"Hi, Ellen," Nancy shouted as she suddenly appeared on her porch and began walking down the steps to greet her neighbor.

Nancy was a big woman – certainly, bigger than her husband, Sam – with dark hair. It seemed every day she wore a sweat shirt and baggy pants. Her face was puffy and she had lost all of her womanly shape, even though Ellen guessed she was only in her early 40s. She had been through a lot: taking care of each dying parent as well as her very sick husband, managing family finances the best she could, and raising her son for the most part alone. Ellen came forward to greet her and give her a hug. She reeked of cigarettes.

"We're going to have to leave soon to get to Keith's game," Nancy said. "You know Keith's athletic prowess as a lacrosse goalie is the highlight of Sam's and my life. You probably find it difficult to believe Keith has any athletic ability. Thank goodness one of his teachers, Mr. Fitz, encouraged him in the fourth grade to start playing lacrosse. The sport came easy for him. Surprisingly, his long legs don't get all tangled up after he lunges after a ball. He's taller and heavier than me. Took after his good looking parent you know." Nancy lightly jabbed Sam in the ribs. Mr. Fitz jostled with all the kids on the team and took a particular liking to Keith, sensing the boy's sadness and aloneness."

"Sadness and aloneness?" Ellen asked.

"Yes. There were few kids for Keith to play with, just the girls two doors down whose folks rented your house before you bought it. The one boy in the neighborhood lived directly behind us across the alley. His name was Todd. His parents fought a lot and his dad often hit his mother. Eventually, the couple divorced, and Todd moved away with his mother. We'd see him every now and then, when he visited his dad. But, he wasn't the cute little boy we knew. He and Keith didn't seem to have much in common."

Nodding slightly as she listened to Nancy, Ellen thought, sure that poor kid was sad and alone. An only child, Keith had grown up with a booze drinking, cigarette smoking dad gone most of the time and a serial smoking mom either chained to her computer or tightly bound to the care of one dying parent after the other. For sure, Keith had known little joy growing up. I'm glad that coach got a hold of him. I watch him amble home from school every day.

Nancy went on. "It was Mr. Fitz who Keith sought when he learned of his father's cancer. He sat down with this kind man and told him what was happening. Mr. Fitz told us Keith then, unashamed, wept large noisy tears, drenching Kleenex after Kleenex which Mr. Fitz gave him. He went on to say most boys at that age wouldn't have told anyone what was going on at home. That saint of a man goes to most of Keith's games now. When I saw you talking with Sam I thought it was a good time to tell you, since I won't we at the committee planning meeting tomorrow. Our sales have slowed down some, but not as much as I suspected they would. I think people are really interested in our neighborhood, cool houses and all the Mamie history."

"That's great, Nancy, We are so lucky to have you do the bookkeeping for the tour."

"Oh, it's a nice diversion from doing the books for Easy Appliance Company. I've done them for a number of years now. The job does not pay a lot, but they have been so good to me. Because of computers, I am often able to do my work at home. We have my desk set up in the living room because that room has the best light, and I can spread out. It's unconventional, but we do have a couch and TV in there, too. When I saw you out here, I wanted to give you the good news, so to speak, about our sales. They could have stopped, you know, Ellen."

Just then Kelly and Yah-Yah Girl came out of their house, headed to their beat-up, dirty vehicles.

"Who is that woman?" Nancy asked when she saw the couple a short distance away.

"That's Kelly's wife or girlfriend who lives with him," Ellen explained.

"Oh, no," Nancy lamented. "He is so good looking. How could he possibly be with that woman? He is so handsome! Kelly used to take such good care of his house. It was always neat as a pin. He'd help Annie, too."

"I didn't know that Nancy," Ellen said. "All I know is the drunken parties Kelly has in his backyard and all the pot smoke and god-knows what other type of smoke. I worry about them making drugs."

"I don't know if the murdered guy had anything to do with drugs." Nancy said. "It is odd, though, because a big drug bust occurred in our alley, I just thought the dead guy might have something to do with drugs. Well, I can't imagine Kelly killing him. Kelly used to be quite strong. Of course, that woman he is with now is big enough to rustle him down," Nancy chuckled.

"Oh, come on Nancy. If that were so, why would they go to the bother of mutilating the body?" Sam carefully articulated.

"Maybe to get back at Axle, a bad guy for sure. I noticed Axle is still at his house, and I had hoped he would be locked up forever. I'll keep you updated. Sorry I won't make the event planning meeting tomorrow. Sam, I am going to close up the house. I'll meet you in back. Bye, Ellen." Nancy said, then turned and walked back up her porch stairs.

"Best get back to my daffodils, Sam," Ellen said and she slowly walked back home, thinking oh good, Nancy won't be there tomorrow. She and her next door neighbor Candy don't get along. Sam did tell me about the day he came home from the hospital. "I had just gotten in bed when Candy next door came bustling in and starting yelling at my wife Nancy for smoking. She screamed, 'How dare you smoke in this house after everything Sam has been through. You are a weak person if ever there was one!' I just went to bed and covered my ears with my pillow. I laid there for days. My dogs never left my side. I was so sick. I threw up all the time from the chemo and radiation."

When she got home, Ellen noticed she had missed cutting off one of the dead flowers. She snipped it with her clippers. Just like the murderer did to poor Hector, she thought.

CHAPTER 9
TOUR PLANNING MEETING
…*LIKE I SAID, WE ALL NEED A LITTLE LOVE…*

Early Saturday morning In her hot red Chevy, Murph pulled up to Ellen's cute yellow house with the black shutters, parked, and hopped out of the car, carrying a big, garish plastic purse and a little white bag.

She knocked on Ellen's front door. Buttercup barked. "Hi, Cuz," Ellen said as she opened the door and eyed the bag.

"Hey, lady. I brought us a couple of chocolate donuts from the box I bought for the office. Saturday is always busy for realtors, you know. Frankly, I'd rather be eating these in my camper in my fishing clothes," Murph wisecracked.

"Oh, Murph. Will you ever just let yourself retire and enjoy life? Your son is quite capable of running your company, you know!"

"That's what you think, lady. If I retired, there would not be any fish left in the Frying Pan River! After the tour, we must spend time in Glenwood Springs so I can go fishing on our way back from your golf tournament in Grand Junction. You can read a book, knit or spend time in the hot springs pool while I am in the stream, catching really big ones!"

After Murph sat down at the kitchen table and gave Buttercup a little forbidden bite of chocolate donut, Ellen brought over two Melmac cups filled with coffee and playfully scowled at her cousin for feeding the dog.

"Boy, Murph, do you believe I was in the Teasing Tigress? Guess what? BB's office walls are actually one-way mirrors. You know, the kind where you can see out, but no one can see in. I've been in lots of those rooms when the advertising agency I was working with was testing various phrases we were considering for television ads. I sure can see why BB would have her office surrounded by them. And, one of her bouncers escorted me to and from her office."

"I sure wish I could have been there, Cuz. Did you find out anything interesting? Is she going to spring any money for a sponsorship?"

"Yes. She agreed to a nice little amount and appreciated our sensitivity for using her company name – not Teasing Tiger – in our sponsorship list. But, Murph, I found out something really awful about Axle." Ellen lowered her eyes and for a couple of minutes was afraid she was going to start crying.

"Oh, lady. What is it?"

Slowly Ellen regained her composure. She blew her nose, and raised her eyes to heaven as she sometimes did when really tough stuff came her way.

"You can't believe the story BB told me about Axle. What a horrible piece of injustice he had at such an early age. He sure did not come from a good family."

"Well, he does get mad really easily. I bet he is full of anger, Ellen."

"Murph, he saw his dad kill his very pregnant mother in front of some of Axle's little brothers and sisters, while his older brother tried to stop his father. Then, the brother grabbed the big long butcher knife they used on the farm out of his father's hand. He stabbed him. The knife went through him and got his mother. BB didn't say if the mom died from a stab wound or trauma. When he realized he stabbed his mother, too, the brother fatally killed himself! Shortly after, Axle came home, his little brothers and sisters were in the yard and told Axle what happened. Axle was afraid the cops would accuse him of the three murders so he took the family car, which was a lot speedier than his truck, and drove as fast as he could to get out of the state. The cops eventually got him, and he was charged with stealing the family car and not sure what else and sent to jail. I forget what state this was in. Poor Axle. No wonder he does not drink, Murph. His dad was a real boozer."

Both cousins lowered their heads. They were consumed by the injustice of it all.

"Hector's death seemed so obvious, at first, didn't it," Ellen quietly said as she got up to refill their coffee cups.

When she came back to the table, she said, "And Murph, BB told me she gave Axle money to start his business. She told me in not so many words that she and Axle had a thing going for awhile."

"No, Ellen. Women like that I think are either married and in the business strictly for money, or their hearts have to be so hard they can't let anyone get to them."

"I'd agree with you, but she said the strangest thing to me, Murph. She said, 'even tough ol' broads need a little love or maybe the illusion of love!' Then, she had the gall to say 'I'd be careful, Ms. Lane. You're pretty and skinny. I would think there would be a "Mrs." in front of Lane. I'd be careful, Ms. Lane. Like I said, we all need a little love.'"

"Well, lady, what can I say? I'm afraid to tell you I agree with her. You may get out your rolling pin and hit me. But before you do, Ellen, I have a few things to tell you, and then I have to boogie out of here and get to the office. Sorry I can't make the tour planning meeting. I hope the ladies understand weekends are super busy for realtors. I do have a box of donuts for them."

"I talked with Javier last night. He told me the Hispanic community is saddened by the death of Hector because he took such great care of his mom. But listen to this, Cuz, Javier has a few connections with drug dealers in the community. He told me he went to school with these guys and finds it helpful for his business to know what is happening in the entire community, and these guys even buy houses from him. Well, he is checking with a few. Then, he told me there has always been a suspicion Hector worked for Jesus even though Hector wasn't caught in the raid in your alley. Javier will be getting back to me."

"Wow, Murph. I can hardly wait to hear what you learn. I'll walk out to your car and get the donuts. I'm sure the committee will be interested in any updates we have about the murder. But, I'm just going to say, we will stay in touch with the cops and will let them know of anything as soon as we do."

Murph replied, "Oh, yes. We sure don't want to start any rumors or amp up the fear."

Later that morning the members of the Pink Blossoms Garden and Neighborhood Tour committee arrived at Ellen's home.

The first to arrive was architect Betty Nobel. She came in carrying a traveler box of coffee in one hand and an expensive-looking, light brown briefcase in the other. "Ellen, dear, it's so amazing you are still hosting us today after ….." Her voice trailed off as she put the box on Ellen's kitchen counter.

"Yes," chimed in Sarah Ferrell, a teacher at Englewood High School, who followed her in the door.

Englewood's Community Relations Manager Karen Sanders was right behind her. "Oh, Ellen, you have tried so hard and are doing such a good job for this tour."

Finally, Ellen's neighbor, pudgy Candy Wallace, a nurse, arrived. "I left Cutie home. I didn't want her to eat all of our donuts, ladies" Everyone laughed.

"Well, ladies," Ellen said. "Thank you. But really, the tour is so important for our community and it has helped me keep my mind off things. I am so glad you are here today. Let's get some refreshments in the kitchen and then come back to the living room to catch up where we are on this wonderful event."

After grabbing their goodies and settling into their seats, Sarah piped up, "But really, Ellen, you must let us know what is happening with the investigation. My teams of moms and kids are a little worried about their safety."

Betty piped up, "Yes, we do need to know what's going on. My team of tour guides from the Colorado Association of Women Architects is wondering if we should even have the tour. If we do, they want to rearrange the route so it does not begin on your block."

"Well, I can tell you," Candy excitedly informed the group. "My team of nurses – we are now calling ourselves The Pink Poodles and Bangs Brigade – is a little scared, but our respective hospitals – all sponsors, mind you – would be a little miffed if the tour was called off. We are having such fun with this. We are planning on having our hair cut so we can have bangs like Mamie, wear poodle skirts, anklets, and saddle shoes, and get this, ladies, maybe even dye some of our dogs pink – like they did in the fifties. Remember, not everyone will have or want a tour guide and our group will be out there if they need help on the route."

"Ladies, ladies," spoke up Karen Saunders. "Our Englewood police force is doing everything they can to solve this mystery as quickly as possible. By the way, Ellen, did you know Mary, or should I call her, Murph, sold Officer Green and his wife their home? Yesterday he mentioned to me he had been thinking of calling her to put the house on the market. It's been about a year since his wife Shae died of breast cancer."

"Oh, no, I didn't," Ellen said. "He or Murph might have mentioned it, but I am not hitting on all cylinders the past couple of days. He seems like such a kind man. I'm sorry. I will let Murph know. Ladies, let's get down to business. First, I have good news from Cathy, our bookkeeper and web master. Our sales are steady! This is definitely something to celebrate. Her son has a lacrosse meet today. That's why she could not share all the details with us. Murph brought us the donuts and wanted you to know she wished she could be here, but Saturdays are the busiest day of the week for realtors."

Karen interrupted, "Sorry to take the floor, Ellen, but I do think Betty has a good idea to begin the tour on another street. That way, people's minds may not automatically think about the murder, or – heaven forbid – even want to go down the alley to see where it occurred."

"Oh, good grief, Karen!" Sarah said. "That is a good point, but I never thought people would want to see the crime scene. I guess they often do, though. My moms and kids are excited about the pink aprons we will give them to wear. I think it helps them re-focus on the purpose of their work. They are so looking forward to getting more history books – and architectural books – thanks, Betty – for their libraries. But, of course, they are worried about their safety. Karen, can we get some police presence?"

Ellen tried to refocus the group and said, "They might be getting some play equipment, too, if Murph is successful with the sponsorship requests she is still making. Candy, I love the name of your group, The Pink Poodles and Bangs Brigade.

"Yes," the rest of the group chimed in.

"You know getting your hair cut so you can have Mamie's bangs takes real guts," Betty added, fluffing up her own brown bangs.

Ellen said, "Candy, I know your shift starts soon as the hospital. Why don't we get together late tomorrow afternoon, maybe for some wine? I do have a few concerns about dogs being dyed pink. I just don't know if that is politically correct now or if it is even legal. We sure don't want to take away any of the focus on your efforts."

"Oh, Ellen, anything for a glass of wine. I'll be over tomorrow," Candy stated as she got up to leave the group.

After she left, Sarah said, "I'm sure glad you said something to her, Ellen. We sure don't want any animal activists to get after us. We have worked so hard."

The rest of the group agreed with her.

Betty announced, "Ellen and I are on working on the script for the guided tour and information on the sheet for people wanting to take the tour themselves. Of course, we are including information on the pink crabapple trees. You know, ladies, just as a side note, this area used to abut a prairie. Except for houses around Denver's downtown area and golf courses, there were few trees here. Planting all those crabapple trees during Mamie's time, certainly added to our green canopy. Today they also help with our air pollution problem caused by all our cars. We will also add information about the horizontal plane of the houses, the use of wrought iron on the porches, and the use of flagstone on some of the houses. Ellen's porch, with her wrought iron railing, is a great example."

"Betty, will the scripts have pictures and can we have sheets at the fudge stations in case we get any questions?" Sarah asked.

"We will certainly have pictures. What a great idea, Sarah, to have information at the fudge stations. What a wonderful opportunity to educate kids about architecture and landscape design."

Looking at her watch, Ellen said, "Our time is about up. We sure covered a lot today. Please watch your emails. I will keep you informed about our progress and any updates from the police. Karen, I know I can count on you to help me coordinate information with the city of Englewood."

"Yes," Sarah responded. "We'll stay in touch, ladies. I am confident our tour is going to be quite a success." She and the other ladies got up, put their coffee cups and plates in the kitchen, and departed Ellen's home.

After they left, Ellen let Buttercup in the house and then collapsed on her couch. Buttercup put her head on her knee, and Sweetie Pie suddenly appeared and jumped in her lap. "Oh, dear, dear," Ellen exclaimed out loud to her beloved pets. "I am so worried about the tour. I can't help but think about Axle and now, I've learned Officer Green lost his wife. Well, my dear friends, I am going out to the garden to do some work. Then, I'll make my favorite dinner, spaghetti, and go to bed early."

Ellen did just that. As she drifted off to sleep, she heard an eerie wailing scream, coming from the alley.

Waking up, Ellen felt every nerve in her body was on fire and starting to poke out of her skin. Her throat tightened. She reached for her glasses and frantically put them on. Sweetie Pie bounded off the bed, and Buttercup woke up with a snort, looked at her, closed her big brown eyes again and drifted back to sleep. Oh God, she thought. I'm probably just dreaming one of those horrible dreams again. That scream seemed so real. I could hear the anguish, grief and torment resounding in it. Yes, I never knew when my alcoholic husband's mood would shift, and he would yell and blame me for everything. I know out of frustration and pain, I screamed just like that scream I heard   in   my   dream.

CHAPTER TEN
KELLY AND COMPANY
… THE ANGUISH, GRIEF AND TORMENT I SUFFERED WHEN A MRS. WAS IN FRONT OF MY NAME…

As she slowly woke Sunday morning, Ellen *thought oh, the anguish, grief and torment I suffered when a Mrs. was in front of my name. What a bad dream. No honey, I remember the scream I heard came from alley. Was it a dream or was it real?*

Buttercup stood up, draped her big front paws on the bed and gave Ellen a big kiss. Ellen said to her beloved Airedale Terrier, "Oh, you big love. Thank you. Yes, it was a bad night and yes, I will get up and feed you!"

After taking care of both Buttercup and Sweetie Pie, she made her breakfast and ate it while writing her daily letter to the "Universe." She asked for help and guidance in dealing with her neighbor Candy and her idea of tinting pink the fur of her dog and dogs of other members of The Pink Poodles and Bangs Brigade. Ellen thought, boy that is a darling name they have come up with for themselves. I love how they are bringing a distinguishing feature of Mamie – bangs – into the tour and the poodle skirts, anklets and saddle shoes. I sure am uncomfortable about the idea of dying the fur of their dogs. I wonder if it is even legal. Now I am worried about dogs standing on the corners with them. What if some kid gets bit?

Ellen made herself another cup of coffee and brought it to the living room. Sitting down on her couch, she remembered the first day she met Candy. The pudgy nurse lived three houses to the north from her on the corner of Emerald Street and Smith Avenue. Yes, it was a day or two before my big moving day, Murph and I had strolled up the sidewalk to the front porch for the final walk through. Wow, what an antiquated rite of passage that is. It is still built into the process of buying a house to make sure the sellers really had done everything stated in the final contract. We had barely entered the house when this short plump woman wearing capris and a sunhat over her corn-silk colored, wispy baby-fine hair yelled at us, 'Well, hello new neighbor. I want to see your house! I'll leave Cutie, her small chubby poodle, outside.' I was stunned – no pissed - by the rude and brazen behavior of this woman who introduced herself as Candy. She told us she had lived on the corner for over 20 years. 'I'm just dying to see this house. I am so proud of my block. People are really starting to take care of these houses,' she announced as she scrutinized each room. I so wanted to tell her to get out, but decided it was not a neighborly thing to do.

Ellen continued to think about her meeting with Candy as she got up and went to her room to dress. I'll get nowhere if I tell her she can't have pink poodles with her brigade. I'll tell her my concerns, and then let her take responsibility for the decision she makes.

About 4 p.m., Candy showed up on Ellen's porch and rang the doorbell. "Hi, Candy. Busy day at the hospital?" Ellen asked as she let her in, thankful she left Cutie home.

"All the days are busy, Ellen. Let's head to your patio and have that wine you promised. I brought over a concoction one of the nurses gave me today. She said her grandmothers used to make it in the fifties. We can snack on it with our wine. She said she would give me the recipe. I think it is basically Chex cereal, peanuts, pretzels, and crackers mixed with Worchester sauce and margarine. Then it is browned in the oven. It might be just the thing to have at our celebration party."

"Sure, Candy. I remember my mom making something like that. It was delicious. What a grand idea to have it at our party. But I am not sure you want to visit on my patio and drink wine because there's a party going on at Kelly's house. People have poured in all day bringing food, booze and a who- knows-what assortment of drugs. Loud country western music is blaring, and Kelly is beating on his drums. The cigarette and pot smoke is so thick it looks like caramel cookie batter dripping down into my yard. Strong whiffs of other smoke are swirling around the cookie batter too, like adding the smell of molasses to the dough. Not sure what it is - pipe smoke? Maybe other types of drugs you smoke? Candy, do you know if methamphetamine smells? It affects Buttercup, too. I don't think this second-hand smoke is good for her, and I don't like her fur reeking of it. So poor Buttercup doesn't get to play in her yard at will, just in the morning when there's not a party going on."

"Let's stay inside, Ellen. I hate smoke, and I hate what has become of Kelly. Maybe we can sit at your kitchen table. I just love what you did to this kitchen."

"We could do that, but might get distracted by Yah-Yah Girl if she comes near her kitchen window."

"The window, Ellen?

Both women stood by the window over Ellen's new white apron sink. Candy remarked, "Oh, I see it is really gray with smoke film, but I can see all those booze bottles of various shapes and colors. And, wow, a wishbone is propped in one of them!"

"It's odd. I have never seen Yah-Yah Girl at the

sink or stove. When I do see her, she is a standing profile yakking at a man. Behind her hangs an art picture of an alluring woman with dark hair and bright pink lipstick, a print or poster which might have promoted a singer or an actress. Do you see it, Candy? I am wondering if Yah-Yah Girl has a glamorous past? I can tell you brooms, mops and dusters have never graced Yah-Yah Girl's hands."

"Oh, I see what you mean. It could be her. Maybe she was a singer at one of Kelly's gigs."

Candy moved to the other window in the kitchen. From there, she could see Kelly's patio. His patio was a hoarder's delight. Chairs, tables, tools, trash cans and boxes were everywhere. A large bar with bar stools was in the middle and stage lights were strung across the width. This clutter did not bother Kelly at all. He was partying with lots of others who didn't mind the mess, either. He stopped drumming, and Ellen and Candy heard him singing a few phrases from "Mammas Don't Let Your Babies Grow Up to Be Cowboys." Smoking and boozing everyday definitely had affected Kelly's voice – low, mumbled, slurred. It seemed to emanate from a hillbilly country singer. A couple of people clapped. "Hey, hey, hey," answered Kelly using guttural growls for emphasis and affirmation. Maybe the sounds were just large burps coming up from all the beer he had drunk.

With the music going, the smoke blowing, and beer flowing, a tall handsome man arrived on the patio and slammed Kelly on the back.

"Candy, do you know who he is? I'm wondering if he is Kelly's brother. I heard he had one. I see him at the house often. He drives a big white panel truck."

"Yes, that's his older brother, Pat. Kelly and

81

Pat's parents died in a car crash when they were little. I think Kelly and Pat had a good upbringing at their Granny's house. Kelly and his ex- wife paid Pat for his share of the house after their Granny died. Kelly told me he didn't want Pat around his wife even though Pat was his brother. Pat has a condo not far from here. Granny used to have a swimming pool in her backyard, and Pat and Kelly used to have jam sessions around it. Drove the neighbors crazy!"

How strange, Ellen thought. Pools are expensive to build and maintain and this was definitely a working-class neighborhood when Pat and Kelly were kids. Here you were lucky to use the pool four months of the year. Snow is not unusual in May and September. Oh my, I remember it snowed on the last day of school when I was in fourth grade!

Candy's next statement brought Ellen back to the conversation, "Granny died after Pat joined the Marines and went to Bosnia."

"Did Kelly join the Marines, too, Candy?"

"Oh, he started a band and was busy playing in clubs in Denver. That's where Kelly met his wife. Pat was married after he got out of the Marines, but it did not last very long. I think he was a tree trimmer and then got a job as a mechanic with the Ford dealership in Englewood. He knows Kelly has a little drinking problem, and I think he keeps an eye on him and tries to help out where he can."

"Well, I don't know about helping Kelly with his drinking problem. I can tell you now that I know who he is, I see Pat here almost every day. With Kelly's throaty, sexy voice, I think he could get a job as a disk jockey or do voice-overs for radio or television advertisements. How do you know all this about Pat, Candy?"

"When I am walking Cutie, I visit with lots of

people. I always stop and talk to Pat when I see him; after all, I've known Pat and Kelly since they were teenagers. But back to Kelly and his drinking, Ellen. I don't think Kelly can get a job at this point in his life because a job would mean he would have to show up at a specific time. I'm guessing his internal clock is operated by his addictions, not by when he needs to get to work. Being a nurse, I know lots of those guys, like Pat who served in Bosnia. You know our neighbors, Brent and Sam, served, too. They try and drown out the memories with booze and whatever. Lots of them come to the emergency room. It's not uncommon for us to see spouses or whoever they live with come in too because these vets often abuse those they love. Some studies show violent behavior may be a way for them to manage unpleasant feelings or release tension, stemming from the many traumatic events they either saw or were involved in."

"I did not know Sam was in Bosnia, Candy. I have had lots of conversations with him, and he never mentioned it. I can see where his job as a truck driver might have been helpful for him. He could drink away from home in an effort to avoid all those horrible things he saw over there. I don't think I have ever talked to Brent, the guy who lives behind him."

"Yes, I know it was really hard on Nancy to deal with all she had to deal with and not have support from her husband most of the time. Even though I have my troubles with her, I can sympathize with the life she has had so far. I really don't know Brent. I just know from what I have heard he doesn't seem to do so well in marriage. It was awful when his son Todd died."

Standing up, Ellen said, "Yes, Sam and Brent and their families certainly have known calamity. Let me pour you another glass of wine, Candy. We can go sit on my couch and talk about your brigade. God, I love the name."

After they settled on the couch and had a couple sips of wine, Ellen told Candy her concerns about the dogs. "Well, if it will make you feel better, I will see if it is legal to safely tint our dogs pink. After all, we are all nurses and would not do anything that would harm our pets. And our poodles will be wearing pink rhinestone collars and leashes, so we will have control of them at all times. If kids come and pet them, we'll be fine. We can always pick up a poodle if need be, unlike a big Airedale, Ellen." Both of the women laughed at the thought of picking up Buttercup, who weighed over 80 pounds.

"Okay. I'll leave it up to you and your bangs and poodles brigade to handle all of this."

Candy handed Ellen her glass and Ellen escorted her to the front door. They hugged and said goodbye.

Ellen went back to her kitchen and poured herself another glass of wine.

I have to get out of this house for a while. Candy drives me crazy, Ellen thought.

Even though it was smoky and noisy, she went to her patio and sat down in one of her wooden chairs.

She heard Pat loudly state, "Yea, the cop came and talked to me. I told him I had no reason to kill the guy, and I thought Axle was a detestable dude who lived behind my brother. I didn't tell him I knew a guy who was a tree trimmer, but was really a drug dealer. The cops never suspected him. I'm not about to snitch on my friend."

"That pole up the butt was quite a good goose job," Kelly explained with a huge deep melodic chuckle.

"Yah," said Yah-Yah Girl. "What wretched screaming I heard coming from the alley last night. I sure as heck will not put up with that behavior again."

For the first time, Ellen felt some empathy for the woman. Apparently, Yah-Yah Girl had loved someone too, who, in the end, betrayed her and his proclamations of always loving and protecting her. What betrayal it is when all of a sudden the man you love turns on you. Yes, Yah-Yah Girl too personally knew how horrible it was to extradite yourself from an abusive love relationship.

Ellen lifted herself out of her chair and went inside. She realized she was very, very tired, but knew she needed to eat something before going to bed early. While Ellen heated up a frozen dinner in the microwave, she made a green salad and poured herself a glass of milk. She felt better after eating her dinner. She quickly cleaned up the kitchen, put her pajamas on, and decided she would call McCoy in the morning and tell him what she heard Pat say and about the scream in the alley.

CHAPTER ELEVEN
A GROWLING DOG
... SHE HAD A BAG PACKED AT ALL TIMES...

Buttercup spied Ellen's uncovered elbow hanging over the edge of the bed and slowly gave it several slurpy, sweet doggie kisses.

Ellen's eyes gradually opened to sunlight streaming through her priscilla lace curtains. Leisurely she extended her arm and stroked Buttercup's coarse brown fur.

"Oh, Buttercup, you darling dog. I know it is past time to get up and take care of you. What a good night's sleep I have had, for once," Ellen said as she gradually got out of bed, grabbed her phone and started to listen to National Public Radio.

She put on her robe and slippers and ambled to the back door with Buttercup trotting beside her. After letting the Airedale out, Ellen went downstairs to fill the dog's bowls and take care of her cat's bowls and litter box. Then she went upstairs, let Buttercup in, and started making coffee in her little espresso maker.

A scream on the radio riveted Ellen's concentration. The scream was part of a story about the relationship between post trauma stress disorder and domestic violence and how it was linked to intimate partner abuse more than had been previously understood by researchers. The reporter went on to state how men may use violent and aggressive behavior in an attempt to release tension associated with their emotions which related to traumatic events.

As she pushed the button on her coffee maker, Ellen remembered that's what Candy said yesterday. Now we know PTSD is why women get abused by so many men. Alcohol and drugs sure rev these guys up, too! One of my poor neighbors, obviously from the scream I heard the other night, is in the throes of this. Gee, I hope she gets out, and gets out soon.

After finishing her breakfast and her daily letter to the "Universe," Ellen was about ready to call Captain Mark McCoy when her phone rang.

It was the volunteer supervisor of the fudge sale. "Hi, Ellen. Sarah here. I know it is early, but I wanted to catch you before my class starts. I haven't been able to reach Joan Broderick about the fudge table she was going to have on her block behind your house. I was wondering if you could check with her later today. I think she might work, but I am not sure," the teacher stated.

"Sure, Sarah. I was going to walk our tour route today to double-check the script Betty Nobel and I wrote for the tour guides. You know we altered it after our meeting Saturday. So it will be no problem at all to stop at Joan's. Her little girls are darling. Have a good day!"

After hanging up, Ellen thought I wonder if I even know Joan. I have talked to her little girls when Buttercup and I have walked by them. Also, I've seen her husband in his garage from time to time, and I saw him help Axle cut down the tree that fell on the fence between their houses. But I can't remember ever talking with her. I can stop by after I finish the route. If she works, maybe she will be home by then. I best get on with my day, but first I have to call McCoy.

She was surprised when McCoy answered his own phone. "McCoy here."

"Hi, McCoy. This is Ellen Lane. I wanted you to know about a few things that may be important for the investigation."

"Oh, great, Ellen. What do you have?"

"Well, first our tour committee decided to change our route so people would not get curious or scared about the murder if it started on my block. Some members felt participants might even go down the alley and search for my garage and driveway instead of focusing on the architectural and historical aspects of our neighborhood. The architect on our committee, Betty Nobel, and I have made some changes. Later today I am going to walk the new route when I take Buttercup out. I'll send you our new route once it is finalized."

"Thanks. Yes, it is always amazing to me how people want to see a crime scene."

"Then, Saturday afternoon, I actually sat on my patio. It was a lovely spring day, but -- of course -- I had to put up with the smoke and stench and noise from next door. Well, while I was out there, I heard Kelly's brother Pat say he lied to the policeman who came to interview him about the murder."

"What did he say?"

"That he lied about knowing the name of the tree trimmer who was a drug dealer."

"Mmmm. That's interesting. Thanks for letting me know. What else did he say?"

"Well, he did not say anything else that would be of interest to you. But the woman who lives with his brother – you know I call her 'Yah-Yah Girl' –talked about the woman's scream that came from the alley Friday night."

"The scream, again?"

"Yes, I heard it, too. When I heard Yah-Yah Girl talking about it, I knew I wasn't dreaming. I heard it as I was drifting off to sleep. It was eerie and haunting. At first, I thought I was having a bad dream about my former husband. In my bones, my very essence, I knew the scream was about -- despair and hopelessness. When I was married, I had a bag always packed and left several times. Yah-Yah Girl said she heard the scream too, and knew the woman was being abused because she used to scream like that before she had gotten out of a violent relationship, too."

"I see, Ellen. So you suspect one of your neighbors is being abused?"

"Yes."

"Can you tell me which direction it came from?"

"I wish I could. But I was too groggy with sleep to focus. I can tell you a couple of hours ago I heard on NPR a story about PTSD and the link researchers have discovered to 'intimate partner abuse,' as they put it. Several of my neighbors are old enough to have been in the thoughtless wars of late. So maybe it was one of them."

"Very interesting, thank you. Please call me again if you hear or see anything more."

"I will, Officer McCoy. Please let me know if you are going to release to the media the cause of death or even the autopsy report. Any news you can give me will be helpful to get out quickly to our committee."

"Sure will, Ellen. Thanks for calling."

Just then McCoy's secretary came into his office followed by Inspector Green. She told her boss, "Got the autopsy back, McCoy. You may be relieved to know Hernandez was probably unconscious when the murderer took the buzz saw to his neck!"

"It wasn't a buzz saw," McCoy retorted. "It was an alligator lopper. The murderer had to get both blades around his neck – like an alligator taking a huge bite!"

"Oh McCoy, do you have to be so graphic?"

she said. "And the pole up his butt was just for decoration. He was gone before that happened, too!"

"Wow," thought McCoy.

"Also," she stated, "He had hardened arteries, probably wouldn't have lived much longer. Want to know what he had for breakfast?"

"Egg burritos," he replied.

"Nope, honey nut cheerios with whole milk and a banana!"

"Oh, so healthy," McCoy responded.

"And," Green exclaimed, "guess what we found in his pocket?"

"A condom," McCoy smirked!

"Funny guy! A little bit of white powder, and we don't think it is laundry detergent. We're having it analyzed right now," Green concluded.

After they left his office, McCoy pondered what to make of the report. He thought drugs, huh! I've wanted to interview Ellen's neighbor to the south for a long time because I suspect he may be manufacturing something. Maybe I should go visit him now while it is still morning, and he isn't too drunk and stoned yet. I wonder if guys like that ever get hangovers. God, I hate them. They are the reason I watch my drinking! While I am at it, I think I'll go talk to brother Pat, too. I know we have already talked to both of these guys, but I want to interview them personally.

McCoy tipped back in his chair and continued to think yes, this has the makings of a drug case alright. But it seems so strange Hector was murdered in this particular alley and in Olde Englewood, to boot. Yep, I think I should get Dungaree to help.

He got out of his chair, left his office and climbed two flights of stairs to the third floor where Dungaree had his office. His real name was Michael Drysten.

He was crusty and old, but a darn good forensic investigator. Maybe the best in the Rocky Mountain area. Often Dungaree was called upon by other jurisdictions to help on investigations because he just seemed to have a nose for finding out vile facts that led to the apprehension of murderers. The trick, though, was to motivate him to help. He was in his late sixties and really wanted to retire.

McCoy knocked on his door. His office was a small dull room. It was on the north side of the building and always dark and cold. The walls were painted a light gray, and there were bones and skeletons on shelves and hanging from the walls. Next to the door, a black leather coat and a Harris Tweed cap hung on a wooden coat rack. Dungaree was grayer than his walls. Sturdy and strong, maybe 5 foot 10 inches, he was slightly balding with grayish red hair, and was dressed in a gray polo shirt and gray corduroy pants. He was always chomping on something. Today, it was his pencil.

"Hello, Dungaree," McCoy cheerfully said as he entered the older man's office, carrying the Hernandez file.

Dungaree grunted.

"I'm working on a very interesting case and know you can hardly wait to help me solve it. It involves a murdered Mexican with his head nearly severed by an alligator lopper and his guts goosed by a tree pole. Of course, there is the usual stew of alcohol and drugs everyone is involved in. Doesn't it sound like fun, Dungaree?" McCoy concluded with a chuckle.

Dungaree grunted and gruffly said, "Leave, McCoy. Just leave. I am involved in a gruesome case now and don't need another gory murder to work on."

"Oh sorry, Dungaree. You know I can't do that.

If I could, I would. I should have brought you a pint of Highlands Best Scotch and a bouquet of Harrison yellow roses to convince you to help me," McCoy said. He detected a small grin on the old man's face. McCoy knew perfectly well the old Scot had wrestled with alcoholism and hadn't touched a drop of "Highlands Best Scotch" in decades.

"Ok, ok, sit down and tell me all about it," Dungaree said pouring them both a cup of coffee that looked like dark putrid Scottish bog.

"Oh,thanks. I just love your coffee," McCoy sarcastically replied. "Well, the case starts with a call from a small, smart, 60-something woman named Ellen. Seems she found a dead man draped over a large yellow chain she puts up every Tuesday evening to keep trash trucks off her driveway on Wednesday mornings. In order for the drivers to execute a very tight turn on one of the city's peculiar little alleys, they use her driveway."

Dungaree asked, "What's the big deal about that? Why won't she let them use her driveway?"

"Like I told you, Dungaree, this woman is smart. She knows those trucks will wear down her concrete because it is not thick enough to handle their weight."

"I see, McCoy. Not many people know about the correlation between weight and concrete depth."

McCoy stated with a quirky little smile on his face, "When she found him, the guy was obviously dead because blood was draining down his neck across her pristine driveway to a hole in the alley sarcastically called by residents, 'the fishing hole.' It has been carved out by countless turning trucks in that odd-shaped alley. The victim, Hector Hernandez had his green Axle Tree Service shirt on and apparently came to work a little early that day."

Dungaree rubbed his chin and softly said, "My, my, my. What a way to start your day."

McCoy went on, "Ellen has all sorts of characters for neighbors, including the old lady Annie who spotted the drug deal in the alley a couple of years ago, the big guy who operates a tree trimming company, a fellow who lost his voice from smoking and drinking, a next-door neighbor who parties all the time, and one whose kid last year in Englewood caused the fatal accident that killed him and three of his classmates."

"And what about the dead kid?" Dungaree asked.

"Oh, I'm not sure he is a part of this murder or not. I don't want you to get muddled, Dungaree, so for now, I just want you to help me with Hector." McCoy winked at Dungaree, knowing the older man was known for a keenly sharp mind, certainly not one that would be muddled.

"Smarty," Dungaree retorted. "And is there something you can't figure out about Hector? You, McCoy, really," he returned the wink.

"Well, for one, I don't know where he has been living since his dear mother departed this earth several years ago, nor do I really know how he fed himself since he quit the restaurant where they had worked for years."

McCoy got up, handed him the case file to review and walked out the door.

Intrigued by this death, Dungaree decided to go to the funny little alley later that afternoon.

* * *

About an hour before Dungaree left his office

to survey the murder scene, Ellen put on Buttercup's leash, put a small map of the proposed new tour route and her house key in one of her jean pockets, her garage remote control and a doggie poop bag in another, and headed out the front door.

As she was walking, she fondly remembered the many neighborhood walking tours the nonprofit she started had done over the years. Working closely with the Colorado Association of Women Architects and numerous neighborhood associations, the Old House Society's tours always attracted several hundred participants. While most of the tours were in older neighborhoods, several of them focused on areas built after World War II. These featured the now-popular mid-century architecture. An avid gardener, Ellen always made sure the tour guide's script included information about the landscape architecture of the time, too.

She noted the many special features of the mid-century built homes she passed. All of them were ranch style and many of them were brick. Numerous brickyards had been built in the Denver area for two reasons: the material to make bricks was readily available thanks to the Rocky Mountains; and because of the late 1800's brick ordinance required all buildings be built from brick or stone after a deadly fire destroyed hundreds of buildings. Decades later, even though the ordinance was repealed, many homes had brick exteriors. In the 1950s, the blond-brick ranch style with some flagstone trim was very trendy.

Wood frame houses were cheaper and faster to construct. So along the route Ellen was taking, houses built out of both brick and frame could be seen. Most of them had iron railings and columns on the front porch with stone or brick planters. Corner windows were popular.

Petunias, particularly the variety called "pink ballerina," graced the planters and kidney-shaped gardens on the front lawn. Most of the homes had at least one pink crabapple tree.

The Broderick's home was near the end of the tour. It had blond brick with red brick trim and a front porch with a black wrought iron railing and columns. It was after 4 p.m. when Ellen walked by with Buttercup in tow.

Doesn't look like anyone is home. I think I'll turn back and go through the alley to my house. Maybe I'll see Brent in his garage and ask him when Joan will be home, Ellen thought.

Walking down the narrow cement alley that led to the back of her house and the intersection with the dirt alley, Ellen's stomach started to churn. She thought, oh dear, will I ever get over thinking about finding Hector Hernandez?

She turned when she came to the main alley and saw Brent's garage door was open. "Come on, Buttercup. Let's go meet Brent. I have never talked with him."

Ellen walked up to Brent's garage and said, "Hello."

Brent looked up from working on his car and glared at her. "What do you want? Aren't you the one who puts up the chain and caused all the commotion last week?"

He walked towards her. Buttercup started to growl. "Get that beast away from me," he hollered.

Ellen, stunned by his behavior, abruptly turned around to go back to her home, but Buttercup growled even louder at Brent and would not follow Ellen. Feeling terror, she saw Brent's blood-shot eyes and raised arm. Ellen pulled Buttercup as hard as she could, but the dog would not budge. Brent was almost upon them.

Suddenly, a man wearing a black leather coat and a tweed cap was at her side. He gently, but firmly, grabbed her hand that held the leash and said, "Here, let me help. Those Airedales can be so stubborn!"

Buttercup calmed down immediately and allowed the man to guide her.

Brent called out an obscenity and retreated to his garage.

Ellen fumbled in her jean pocket and finally pulled out her remote garage control. Pushing the button, the garage door opened. The couple and dog went in.

Turning to the man, she said "Thank you. I think that man was going to hit my dog! She wouldn't come because she was trying to protect me."

She began to shake and the man gently put his arm on her shoulder.

Quivering she asked, "Who are you?"

"I'm Chief Inspector Michael Drysten of the Englewood Police Department."

Staring into Ellen's lovely hazel eyes, he added, "Most people call me Dungaree."

CHAPTER TWELVE
A BUSY DAY FOR THE COPS
... *COULD THIS HARDENED MAN BE CAPABLE OF CRYING?* ...

Green got into his car and headed to Bolton's coffee shop on Hampton, a place frequented by cops. He needed a good cup of joe.

He had a meeting with Murph in 30 minutes to discuss his housing needs, now that he was a widower. He also wanted to find out anything she and Ellen had turned up about the murder. Since a statement from the police department would go to the press within the hour, he wanted to tell Murph what Hector's autopsy showed.

The extra time would help him calm himself down. It was still hard to talk about Shae's death from breast cancer. When they were looking for houses with Murph, she always had been so accommodating to his schedule and had many times met Shae and him at this coffee shop.

Stella Bolton was behind the coffee bar herself today. She had operated and owned the shop for 10 years. Green figured she had been around the block a few times – hadn't we all! Stella was pleasant and her food and coffee were edible.

"Hi, Dan! How's it going?" She took a good look at him. "Your usual, then?"

"Yeah. Thanks, Stella." She handed him a large cup of coffee and a chocolate covered donut. Before leaving the counter he put a couple of spoons of sugar in the coffee and dumped some cream in it, too.

You can always tell folks from back East – even Midwest by how they doctor up their brew, Stella thought.

Green was grateful the morning crowd had gone without eating the last chocolate donut. He went over to a table by the window. A local paper's sports section was spread out. Nothing he didn't already know from the radio and his phone. He thought *thank goodness newspapers don't have the staff they used to have. Hector Hernandez' picture and story would have been the news of the day for a while, gory pictures and all. Now, they would probably just print the department's news release.*

He took a couple of deep swallows from the coffee and devoured most of the donut. Where do we go from here? he thought. The white stuff in Hector's pocket is heroin. The news release identifies it only as an illegal drug.

Green looked out the window and saw Murph drive up in her sporty red car. He had always thought of her as middle-aged; however today, watching her get out of the car, Green realized she was an older woman. When Murph entered the coffee shop, Green got up, walked over to the smiling woman and escorted her to his booth by the window.

"So good to see you, Murph," Stella said as she poured her a cup of coffee. "If I remember correctly, you just take it black."

"That's right, Stella. I come from a long line of tough Colorado cowboys, so I don't water my coffee down," she winked at Dan.

Stella informed her, "Green got the last of my chocolate donuts."

"Oh, that's okay. A cinnamon sugar will be just fine. I don't need all those extra calories from chocolate."

Green and Stella both laughed at the petite woman.

"She probably could eat a whole dozen and not

put on one ounce," Stella said as she went to get the donut and brought it to Murph.

"You know, Murph, I never thought I would be talking to you about getting a smaller home. I always thought Shae and I would need you to find us a bigger one. We had planned on having several kids and a big nice house with a yard for them to play in. I guess it's not unusual for women to get breast cancer at an early age. But we were so surprised when she found a cancerous lump," Green said with tears showing in his eyes.

Murph reached across the table and put her hand on Green's. "I know, Dan. Life is so unfair!"

After a couple of minutes she removed her hand and asked the cop, "What do you have in mind?"

"I was thinking about a condo not far from here. It is convenient to my work and close to highway 285, so I can get quickly to the mountains. I know I need to do this, but it is so hard for me to get rid of Shae's stuff and get the house ready for sale."

"Ah, we'll take it one step at a time, Dan. Let me send you a market analysis of your house, so you know how much you can afford to spend. Your home has gone up significantly since you bought it. Of course, the whole market has gone up. But I don't think you will have any trouble finding a condo to your liking."

"That sounds good, Murph; but what about getting my house ready for sale?"

"No problem. Once you know what you want, I'll come by, and we'll plan together what you need to do. Also, we can figure out what to do with Shae's possessions. When do you want to get started?"

The cop replied, "I'd like to wait until we solve this murder. It is so perplexing. So much does not make sense at this point. This morning, the department is giving the media a statement about the autopsy report. It should be out momentarily, and I wanted to share that with you."

"How interesting. What did the report say?"

"It showed the deceased first received sharp blows to the head and neck. The jugular vein was ruptured. Then, the head was almost decapitated and the pole jammed into his anus. A small amount of an illegal drug was found in a bag in his pants pocket."

Green paused and then went on, "You know, Murph, the drug mentioned is heroin and severe bleeding occurs within minutes after the jugular veins are ruptured. It appears Mr. Hernandez was assaulted near the chain in the driveway because we did not find blood anyplace else. The cause of death adds to the confusion. "

"Wow. So, if he was dead or dying from the jugular being ruptured, why was his head almost cut off?"

Green replied, "We don't know. It appears the killer was making a statement with the body."

"Heroin? Did you find any in his body?" Murph asked.

"No."

"How interesting. Maybe he was going to use it after his shift ended for PU Services. Do you know if he had any friends on the trash truck?"

"We don't. But we are going to check."

"Dan, I have some information you might find useful. I asked a friend of mine who has connections in the Mexican community to see what he could find out about Hector. He was told it was suspected for a long time Hector worked for Jesus, the man busted in Ellen's alley for drug trafficking. However, Hector was not an ordinary worker. The connections thought

Hector had a special role in the company and might have been Jesus' bookkeeper and kinda like an office manager. No one knew where Hector lived after his mom died. They thought Hector might have some sort of administrative role and possibly lived at Jesus' headquarters. No one could confirm this, but no one knew if Jesus had headquarters for sure. If he did, they didn't know the location."

"Boy, Murph, this is interesting information. I don't want to put your friend's life in jeopardy, so I won't ask who it is or who the connections are."

"Thanks, Dan. One other thing, who is Chief Inspector Michael Drysten, also known as Dungaree? My cousin had quite a scare in the alley yesterday, and he came to her rescue."

"We've asked Michael Drysten, who heads up our forensics division, to help us with the case because it is so puzzling. He is known throughout the state for solving difficult cases. I don't know why he was in the alley yesterday; but I do know your cousin was in excellent hands."

Green's phone rang. When he saw who it was, he said, "Murph, I need to go. McCoy needs me."

Murph stood up. Shook his hand and said, "I'll get your house information to you very soon, Dan."

Together they walked out of Bolton's.

Before leaving the parking lot, Murph called Ellen and told her about the autopsy report.

* * *

Green got two cups of coffee from the office canteen area, gave one to McCoy and shut his supervisor's door. McCoy said, "I have an 11 a.m. appointment with Jesus and would like you to come

101

along. Also, I was wondering if you have any news."

"Talked with some gang contacts. General belief out there is Hernandez worked closely with Jesus, but not in the usual way. He was rarely on runs and collections."

"What would he have been doing then?" McCoy asked.

"I'm guessing Hernandez, though not formally educated, had some knowledge of bookkeeping. I found out he took some classes at Arapahoe Community College, bookkeeping and computer skills, like QuickBooks," Green revealed. "My contacts told me he would have been long dead if he had slipped out on a run or a collection or had snitched. I'm thinking that's why we can't find where Hector lived or any tax returns. I'm guessing he lived in a warehouse or an office of some sort, taking care of books and inventory."

Green emptied his coffee cup and went on, "Also, I just had breakfast with Murph to talk about selling my home, and she told me she has a friend with connections who told her the same things I heard from my contacts. Interesting, huh?"

"Well, we do know Jesus had a big operation and was a real entrepreneur. Just expanding out of the customary geographic area shows that. So maybe his headquarters still exists since we have no record of where he lived. Jesus was brilliant to make runs in these quirky little alleys," McCoy stated and then finished his coffee, too. "So, continuing our assumption this is a drug crime, where do we go from here? Who would make such a statement, a warning if you will, with the butchery of the body? Did your contacts give you the names of any big drug dudes who might have done Hector in?"

"No, but we do have a system-wide list of

suspected drug pins. It may be of some help. I'll pull it up later today and see what we get," Green said. "We're going to have to leave soon for the prison to talk with Jesus Reyes, the head of the drug gang, we busted in that alley. How do we go about this interview – finesse if you will? We have to be careful because I don't want to get any of my contacts in trouble."

"Yeah, I've been thinking about that" McCoy responded. "Jesus is going to be in jail so long, I doubt he will go back into business if he ever gets out. My guess is Hector was his one hope of getting a little cash in prison, or maybe shutting down the business so none of his competitors could get his user and supplier contacts. Let's just go in and be gentle, maybe praise him a little for his business acumen. See if he has any emotions for Hector."

"Okay," Green said. They left McCoy's office and drove a couple of miles to the state prison, which was Jesus' home for the next couple of decades.

The big brick dark building, surrounded by a tall barbed wire fence, and look-out towers was an imposing structure to say the least. The cop car came to a halt at the gate, and they had to show their credentials and documentation of an appointment with an inmate. They drove in, parked and walked up the 20 or so concrete and steel steps to the entrance door. Once inside, they went through a security check much stricter than at any airport. The prison superintendent herself, Willa Goddard, met them as they cleared security. She was an old friend of McCoy's.

"Hello, Captain. So nice you have come to visit us today! Would love for you and Officer Green to join me for tea in my spacious office suite after your official business," she teasingly quipped with laughing eyes.

Playfully, McCoy responded, "Why ma'am, we

would be honored to have tea with you. Thank you."

The superintendent introduced them to one of her guards. "Thomas, will take you to the visiting area," she said.

The cops went into a small room and sat down on two uncomfortable chairs with blue padding and chrome legs, in front of a Plexiglas shield. Shortly, the guards brought out a small Hispanic man. He appeared to be about 40, dark hair, stubble on his face and slightly bent over. He wore handcuffs and an orange prison jump suit. Sitting down in a chair opposite the men with the shield separating them, he scowled, and the police thought Jesus detested their whiteness and their badges.

"Hello, Jesus, I am Captain Mike McCoy and this is Officer Green." Jesus looked like he could spit at them. "I suspect this is not something you would like to discuss on such a fine morning, but we're trying to find the killer of Hector Hernandez." Jesus seemed to stiffen a little at Hector's name. "I'm assuming you already know about his death," McCoy said. Jesus nodded. "We understand he worked for you. It seems you had a special relationship with Hector, one of the few people you could truly trust." With that statement, Jesus' eyes closed. "I suspect the nature of his death and the location is disturbing to you."

With this statement from McCoy, Jesus' eyes squeezed shut even more. McCoy wondered if this hardened man could be capable of crying.

After a moment or two, McCoy continued, "The location and manner of death is really curious to us because it is so brutal and not the normal death we see in gang or drug related violence. Generally, these deaths are caused by gunshot or knives. The bodies are not so prominently displayed."

Jesus stared back. McCoy revealed, "We've

extensively interviewed the owner of the tree service company he was working for." The cops noticed Jesus tremble, and he closed his eyes again. "And we are not bringing charges against him. We also interviewed another man who used to be a tree trimmer, and it appears unlikely he is the murderer, though we are curious about a possible drug connection. In both cases, we could not find a motive to kill."

With McCoy's last statement, Jesus' eyes opened, and he briefly looked baffled about the connection to drugs. "Frankly, it just doesn't seem to be gang or drug oriented, and at this point, we don't suspect you for ordering this murder," McCoy stated.

Jesus let out a little growl. The sound seemed to communicate, 'how dare you implicate me.'

"It would be helpful to have a list of possible customers or even suppliers," Green offered, "Or maybe a location where we might find this list." Jesus shook his head 'no.' "Well, sir, in case it comes to mind where we might find that list or anything you think might be helpful, please contact us. Your cooperation could help you get out of here sooner."

With that the cops rang a bell and guards came and escorted Jesus back to where he came from. Thomas also appeared and led the cops to the superintendent's office. Willa had a teapot ready and the three of them sat down and discussed the case and life.

"Nice woman, with a tough, tough job," McCoy said when the men got back into the cop car. He wondered if Green would ever date again. The superintendent seemed like a good choice for him since they were about the same age and in the same profession.

* * *

When McCoy got back to his office, he decided to confirm Hector's employment with PU Services, which they hadn't formally done, and arrange for an interview with Hector's supervisor tomorrow. In his previous role with the city of Englewood, he had already talked to the supervisor about Ellen's complaints.

It was getting late for the corporate types. He called PU Service's head honcho's office and told the secretary who he was. She immediately put him through to Mitch Boyd. "Hi, Mitch – Captain McCoy here. Would like to visit with you in about an hour. Are you going to be around?"

"For you McCoy, I'll clear my calendar. What's this about so I can be a little prepared?" Boyd asked.

"It's about one of your guys who got his head almost lopped off and his rear reamed. I want to verify his employment and get any other information you might have. You might have seen it on the news," McCoy said.

"Yes, I am aware of the murder in the alley. I'll see you soon, McCoy."

After hanging up, McCoy told his secretary, "I am going to spruce up a bit and then go talk to my friends at PU Services in their fancy corporate office. I want to make sure Hector Hernandez worked for them. I'll let you know if I find anything." He walked out of his office and headed to the Denver Tech Center.

At 4 p.m. McCoy sauntered into Mitch Boyd's office and sat down in one of the soft brown leather couches. Boyd's cute secretary brought him a cappuccino and one for Boyd, too. He took a couple of sips, admiring the view of Long's Peak from Boyd's window. McCoy thought as he reached in his pocket and pulled out the gory photo of the dead man. Boy,

Ellen was so right. PU Services really are arrogant. And they make so much money.

"Recognize this guy, Boyd?" he asked.

Mitch took a look and then appeared green. He quickly gained his composure (McCoy was sniggering inside). "Sorry McCoy, I don't. Why would you think I know him?"

"Well, we found him draped over a yellow thick chain on the resident's property in the alley. I think you may recall about the chain. The woman used it to keep your trucks off her driveway," McCoy said.

Bother, Boyd thought. Not that woman – generally we can just bully them a bit, and they go away. She just kept at it. We even hiked her rates and didn't even pick up her can after she cancelled service until McCoy confronted me.

"Really! Our folks don't wear green shirts. Why do you think he is one of ours?" Mitch said evenly, trying to keep his voice and guts under control.

"I interviewed Axle Kutz. He has a tree trimming business directly behind the house of the woman with the yellow chain. The autopsy showed a blow to the victim's head and neck caused the jocular vein to rupture, then an alligator lopper – used to chop big branches – was used on his neck to partially sever the head and there is a tree lopper in his rectum, which you can see in the photo," McCoy answered smoothly.

Watching Boyd grow more and more uncomfortable, McCoy said, "I visited with Axle and he told me the man in the photo came to him for a job on Wednesdays because his employer, PU Services, was changing hours to 10-hour days and he could request which day he did not want to work. He knew about the tree service company because he worked on your truck that collected trash in the alley. Apparently, the man was not too comfortable being yelled at on Wednesdays by the resident with the yellow chain whenever the truck's tire even grazed her driveway, so he asked for that day off."

"I see. Let me do a little research and I'll get back to you," Boyd said as he wobbly stood up and then escorted McCoy to the door. He then went into his private bathroom and threw up.

CHAPTER THIRTEEN
THIS AND THAT AND BROTHER PAT
... THEY WERE ALWAYS SO MAD, BUT SO ASSURED OF THEMSELVES...

When McCoy woke the next morning, his wife Lynn was still sleeping, snuggled up next to him. He loved this woman. Her dark hair, now streaked with gray, fell softly on her shoulders. She had a smile on her face. Their marriage had been a good one. Like now, there just was a "peaceful easy feeling."

Then his reverie was abruptly interrupted by the thought of Hector Hernandez. Wonder who was in his bed when he has waking up? Someone had mentioned he had met a girl. What did the poor guy do to deserve such a violent death? He hoped it came quickly and Hector never felt the blows to his head prior to the alligator lopper chomping down on his neck.

He gave Lynn a soft kiss on her forehead and carefully eased himself out of bed. She moaned. "Sorry I was so late getting home last night – book club, you know," Lynn mumbled.

"Not sure when I will be home, hon. Hernandez case is a tough one," he said as he dashed off to the shower.

McCoy drove to his office and pondered who he should interview first. He'd wanted to talk to Ellen's neighbor to the south, Kelly Buck, for a long time because he suspected him of manufacturing something. Maybe he should go visit him now while it was still morning, and he wasn't too drunk and stoned yet. I wonder if guys like that ever get hangovers? I hate hangovers. They are the reason I watch my drinking!

Before he left to interview Buck, he checked his

emails and found one from Mitch Boyd, with a list of employees for the Old Englewood route and the supervisor contact information. McCoy already knew the supervisor. He had called him several times about Ellen's complaints. McCoy remembered the guy sounded annoyed and snapped his answer, "Okay, Captain. I'll take care of that right away, sir."

He got back to Boyd and requested to see Joe Martinez at their offices when he got off his shift. Boyd called him back and said he arranged for Joe Martinez to meet him an hour before his shift ended at 4 p.m.

McCoy got in his car and drove the five miles over to Kelly's house. He saw the beat-up old white panel truck in front of the house. The front door was open. McCoy walked up the sidewalk. Amazing, he thought – no cracks – they used to make good cement back then.

He knocked on the screen door and saw Kelly open the door in a small hall that looked like a bathroom door to McCoy. Kelly startled, looked up and yelled, "Yeah, what do you want? No one is home!"

"Captain Mark McCoy, Englewood Police Department, Mr. Buck. I'd like to speak with you."

With a scowl, Kelly wiped his eyes and slowly sauntered to the door to open it. "Okay. What's this about?" he said.

"May I come in?" McCoy asked.

"Oh, sure, come right in and sit yourself down!" Kelly sang sarcastically.

McCoy went in and sat on a dilapidated old couch. A huge TV was on the other end of the room. The house stank of booze, cigarettes, pot (which was legal in Colorado residences) and something else, kind of sweet. McCoy supposed it was some illegal drug, maybe the one he suspected Kelly made.

"Thanks, Mr. Buck."

"Knock off the 'Mr.' part. People call me Kelly."

"Okay, Kelly. Just want to make sure you are you aware of the murder that took place in your alley?"

"Yeah – but I did not do it – heard about it from my Ex. She lives up the street and said the alley was completely blocked off when she was trying to get to work that day."

"Well, your neighbor, Ellen," McCoy started to say.

Kelly interrupted him and groaned, "Oh, that old broad! Is she dead? Hallelujah!"

"No, she is not dead, but she found the victim draped over a chain she puts up across her driveway each Tuesday night to keep the trash trucks off her cement driveway."

McCoy decided to describe the crime scene in detail. He hated Kelly's attitude and thought the shock might jolt him a little from the booze and drugs still in his system. "She raised the garage door and saw blood draining off her driveway to the alley to the "hole" by the chain link fence. Some of your neighbors describe it as the local "fishing hole." The man's head had been partially severed off by an alligator lopper. Are you familiar with that tool, Kelly?"

"Nope," he replied in disgust like a teenage boy.

McCoy got out his smart phone and said, "Let me describe it to you, per Black and Decker. But first, I can tell you it looks kind of like an alligator head. You know how good alligators can bite. It says, 'Innovative clamping jaws grab and cut in one easy motion, 6" cutting bar and chain allows for a maximum cutting capacity of 4" lightweight design for ease of use.' It goes on to describe that it is often used to cut thick tree branches, but it did a fine job on the man's neck,"

111

McCoy concluded.

Kelly looked a little green. McCoy decided to continue to see if he could really make him sick. He went on, "Sticking out of his butt was a long tree pole lopper." McCoy looked at his phone again and continued reading the Black and Decker description of the alligator tool, "Technology sets the extra-large teeth on the curved blade at four angles that makes the blade ideal for even the toughest pruning jobs. Adjustable blade provides two angles of cutting power and two sickles: upper and lower.' That's the Black and Decker description on Cabela's web site."

"God, I love that store. You ever go there, Kelly?" McCoy asked and looked up at Kelly, expecting him to be retching.

Instead the grayed man, with the devil goatee, gave a deep melodic chuckle and belched. "What a goose job!" he exclaimed.

"Also, the victim was wearing a green shirt from the tree trimming company, located behind you. We found a little white stuff in one of his pockets – heroin," McCoy said. He seemed to detect a small change in one of Kelly's bloodshot eyes.

"We talked with Axle about the murder, but that's a lot of vengeance for a guy to have for a worker," McCoy said.

"Ever have any doings with your neighbor Axle Kutz, Kelly?"

"Nope," Kelly grunted. "Insurance company wanted me to get a branch off my house last year. I thought about talking to Kutz, but I did it myself!"

"You did?" McCoy asked. "How big of a branch was it?"

"Well, actually my brother and the guy across the street did it. They wanted some money, not as much as what Kutz would charge, and borrowed the equipment from my neighbor's dad."

"You have family in town, then?" McCoy asked.

"Yeah, what's it to you? I have a brother, Pat. Our parents were killed in a car accident a number of years ago." Kelly relayed, his eyes seemed to water a little. It was hard for McCoy to tell though. They were so bloodshot. "Yeah, our granny finished raising us in this house."

"Sorry, man," McCoy said. "Your brother live here in town?"

"Yeah, he has a condo not far from here. My ex-wife and I paid him off for half of this house after Granny died. I didn't want him around my wife even though he is my brother, and we had a kid right away, too." Kelly stated.

McCoy asked, "So your brother and the guy across the street took down the limb?"

"Yeah, and Pat said I should have some of the other branches taken down, so the old broad next door wouldn't get on my back. He did a good job. Trimmed trees for awhile when he got back from the service."

"Well, you were a lucky guy to have a brother that could do that for you!" McCoy said.

"Yep, I guess so. I'm going to get a beer out of the fridge. Want one, McCoy?"

"Oh, thanks, but I got to get going. Thanks for your time," McCoy said and he walked out the door.

* * *

McCoy needed to get the stench from Kelly's house out of his nose and hopefully out of his clothes, and he needed to think. So he drove around the block and parked close to the little cement ally that led into the alley behind Ellen's house. He rolled down his windows and thought, obviously brother Pat had the tools and strength to do the job. I'll see what I can find on my phone about Pat. He opened up his phone. Boy I hate having to put in my pass code every time. The touch ID rarely works. He googled Pat Buck and his phone spewed out a few lines. He hit the White Pages link and an address not far from Kelly's house came up.

McCoy started the car and then noticed Ellen's silver Honda was headed toward him. He rolled up the blackened window. He didn't feel like waving to her today. She came to the end of the alley and turned north. Wonder where she is going, McCoy thought.

After Ellen was out of sight, he swung over to Smith Avenue and then took a left on Santa Fe Drive, a main thoroughfare in Denver, until the interstates were built 50 years or so ago. He drove just past Hampden and pulled into a condo/apartment complex. He noticed a white panel truck in the parking lot, which looked like the one he had seen parked in front of Kelly's house. He parked and then walked up three flights of stairs to Pat's door. It was closed, not open like Kelly's. He rang the bell. He could see an eye peeping at him through the peep hole. "Yeah," a voice said.

McCoy responded, "Englewood Police. I'd like to talk with you."

Pat opened the door. "Please come in, Officer. My brother called and told me you might be stopping by to talk with me," Pat said.

McCoy was taken aback by his kindness and the cleanliness of his house. He noticed only the smell of cigarettes. The house was almost antiseptic. No pictures, no beer cans, no pets – just a respectable looking couch and a television.

McCoy started, "So, Kelly probably told you about the dead man in the alley a couple of days ago."

"Yes," Pat said. "He also told me how he was killed, and you might have questions of me because I have done some tree trimming in my past."

"Well, all of that is true, Pat. It is a very unusual murder. Oh, and I am sorry about the loss of your parents."

"Oh, that was many years ago. Kelly and I had a good upbringing at Granny's house. She used to have a swimming pool in her backyard, and me and Kelly used to have jam sessions around it. Drove the neighbors crazy I am sure. Granny died after I joined the Marines and went to Bosnia," Pat said.

"Why didn't your brother join, too?" McCoy asked.

"Oh, he started a band and was busy playing in clubs in Denver. That's where he met his wife, you know."

"Have you ever been married, Pat?"

"Yeah, one time, but it did not last very long."

"So after you got out of the Marines you were married for a while and what did you do for a job?"

"Well, I did trim trees for a while until I landed the job I have now as a mechanic with the Ford dealership. I like my work and every now and then I find a girl I like," Pat said and winked.

"Well, we found a little bit of white powder, heroin, in the victim's pocket," McCoy said, watching Pat closely.

"Yeah, so what?"

"Well, you know just a couple of years ago, we busted a gang in that very alley thanks to a tip we got from a resident."

"Oh, yeah, I know about that. Annie doesn't have anything else to do all day but stare out her window. It's so sad. Her kids were older than me and

115

Kelly. Look, McCoy. I don't do drugs, and I had no reason to kill that guy. My brother Kelly has a little drinking problem, and I keep my eye on him and try and help out where I can. That's all."

"Just one last question, when you were trimming trees, did you work with anyone or know any tree trimmers who sold drugs?"

"Well, that was before marijuana was legal in Colorado. So yes, I did know some guys who did that. But I don't even remember their names. I tried that stuff a couple of times. It stinks and I didn't get anything from it. So no Mary Jane for me!"

McCoy believed him. Stood up. Shook Pat's hand. Thanked him. Left and drove back home for lunch, hoping Lynn was there.

* * *

Later that afternoon, McCoy went to the PU Services office building. Joe was waiting for him and McCoy could tell he was not in good humor. "It's a pleasure to finally meet you in person, Joe," McCoy said as he extended his hand.

"Likewise," grunted Joe as he shook the cop's hand.

"What'd you say we go down to Mel's, just a couple of blocks away? I imagine you might be a little hungry and thirsty after getting off work," McCoy said. Joe agreed, knowing that you did not argue with cops.

They drove to Mel's, a greasy dive about a mile from the hotsy-totsy corporate park where PU Services was located. Lots of guys and a few women were downing beers. There was a long wooden bar and beat up old bar stools. A big wooden horse head – painted orange with blue eyes was centered in the back of the bar. McCoy thought, thank goodness, the horse's eyes do not light up. And, thank goodness, the horse isn't exactly like the creepy horse statue stationed as you approach Denver international Airport. That horse really freaks me out and lots of other people.

The floor was covered in black and white commercial laminate tiles. The white was gray by now and the owners apparently had long ago given up cleaning it. It was sticky and yellow from beer and booze.

The women in the bar were known to have "been around the block a few times. With the right 'fare' they'd go some more." McCoy felt sorry for them. Such hard women - such hard lives and such abuse they've had - they were probably much younger than they looked.

McCoy ordered a plate of nachos and asked Martinez if he wanted to share a pitcher. Martinez was skeptical but figured it was free food and beer, and he really had nothing to hide. He went to the john and the food and beer were waiting for Joe when he got back.

"Well, before you dive into the food, Joe, I'd like to show you a police picture of the deceased. We showed the photo to Boyd. It was really grotesque. Afraid it really made your boss sick and upset."

McCoy pulled a photo from his pocket. Joe took one look at it and told him the dead man's name was Hector Hernandez. Joe flinched a bit. "He was a quiet guy. How did he die?" Martinez asked.

"Technically, the autopsy showed a blow to the head caused the arteries to rupture. He died, probably before his neck was cut. Ellen Lane found him draped over the yellow chain."

"Oh, yeah, that broad. She's too old and boney to have killed him, though!" Martinez stated.

"Yeah, and not strong enough to lift an alligator

117

lopper to sever part of his head off, nor ram a tree lopper in his rectum!" McCoy relayed. Martinez gasped and choked on part of his nachos. Beer dribbled from his nose and he grabbed his napkin to cover his face. McCoy turned his head from the disgusting site of Martinez.

"Holy Mary, Joseph and Jesus," Martinez cried. "What an awful death."

"Yep!" stated McCoy. "Since he was wearing a pair of blue jeans and a green Axle Tree Service shirt on when we found him, we talked to Axle right away. Seems he had been arguing with your boy over pay, and, of course, had all of the equipment that severed or gorged his body." McCoy said

"Axle?" Joe said. "Wow – I never liked that guy, seemed two-faced to me. Buttering up to the old lady behind him, scowling at that nice guy with cancer up the alley from him and making my truck wait so he could back out. A couple of guys I know had worked for him, but he never paid him," Martinez said, taking a long draw of beer.

"Yeah. He's an odd duck alright. What can you tell me about Hector?"

"Not much," Martinez said. "Hadn't worked for me long. I wish the company would do drug tests and background checks before we hire anyone. But we're lucky to get anyone to work for us, given the nature of our work – stinky, dangerous, rough roads. We pay them fairly well and offer some insurance. But if you can get a job digging ditches someplace, it's better than riding a trash truck." Martinez concluded.

"Don't know much about Hector. Seems he told me he worked or continued to work in a Mexican restaurant – maybe Lupita's – can't really remember. He wanted a day job, too. Don't remember anything about a wife or parents or sending money back to Mexico. I just gave him the safety talk, and he hopped on the truck," Martinez concluded.

McCoy queried, "Did he seem hung over, stoned? What about any bruises or black eyes?"

"None that I remember, Captain. There are so many of them. Like I said, I just give them the talk and then they hop on and go," Joe concluded.

"Well, thanks, Martinez," McCoy said as he slammed some money down on the table. The two men hit the restroom, pissed and left.

So who would kill poor Hector Hernandez and display his body in such an awful way, McCoy pondered as he drove home. This is a real crime of passion. I know of only three things that perpetuates crimes like this – drugs or revenge for love or death. It seemed so obvious at first when I came to that quirky little alley.

CHAPTER FOURTEEN
ELLEN AND THE PRIEST
... COULD ALMOST HEAR THE MILLIONS OF PRAYERS OF ANXIOUS AND SAD MOTHERS WHISPERED IN ITS PEWS ...

Ellen carefully backed her silver Honda from the garage. Ever since seeing the body of Hector Hernandez draped over the chain on her driveway, she felt anxiety each time she took her car out of the garage.

I feel even more nervousness today, probably because I am going to talk to Father Louie at his church, she thought. I helped set up an Al-Anon conference there a couple of years ago.

She turned up the small cement alley and noticed no one was home at Axle's house. She did not see the parked unmarked police car when she got to the end of it and looked both ways before turning left. As she headed her car to Santa Fe Drive, thoughts of her former alcoholic husband flooded her mind. She had been married to him a good 15 years before she realized how much he was drinking when he got home from work. His mood shifts were hard to believe, and he often quickly turned on her and accused her of all sorts of things. She automatically would defend herself, causing a huge fight that went on for hours. Suddenly, the thought of the scream she heard in the alley crossed her mind. *Yes,* I had screamed just like that many times. I screamed out of desperation, and fear and the god-awful feeling of being backed up against a wall with no place to go.

The morning after one such fight she went into her office. She hadn't slept and was haggard to the bone. One of her peers came in and said, "Ellen, you look horrible!"

Oh, God, I so remember that day. It was so embarrassing. I started to cry. The next day she came into my office again, closed the door, and handed me one of Al-Anon's daily readers. Inside was the phone number of the local office. I called, and they told me where meetings were held. I went to my very first Al-Anon meeting that day over my lunch hour. My co-worker was instrumental in bringing me to Al-Anon, which saved my life.

The stoplight in front of her turned yellow and then red. Ellen realized she was at the intersection where you turned to the Teasing Tiger and that she had been lost in her thoughts ever since she had started driving. She would soon need to turn left to get to Father Louie's church.

Perpetual Church was located in the same run-down neighborhood as Lupita's restaurant. Built at the turn of the century by immigrants grateful for safe passage to the United States, it had a few stained windows and a small spire. The humble building had a sense of serenity about it. Ellen walked in the church and was once again struck by its plain beauty. The major stained glass window featured the Nativity. There were wrought iron shelves full of candles, votive lights, most of which were burning. The cross, hung in the center, was stunning in its simplicity. The hanging Jesus seemed peaceful and understanding somehow to the suffering of people who came into the church. Ellen could almost hear the millions of prayers of anxious and sad mothers whispered in its pews. She doubted few if any of those prayers were answered, but hopefully the women, like her, gained a few moments of peace from their efforts. *"Ave Maria, Dios te salve Maria----."*

Father Louie appeared from a door to the side

of the alter. "Hello, Ellen. It's good to see you again. Let's go to my office where we can talk privately." The priest led her down a hall leading to a staircase to the basement. They entered a small room with a coat rack and a few tables, then into a big meeting room painted white, which could use a clean coat of paint, and linoleum squares of black, brown and off-white on the floor, and a small stage area on one of the walls. The room had hosted many wedding receptions, funeral meals, and AA and Al-Anon meetings. The priest walked through that room and then to a door that led to a small corridor. He turned lights on and off as he went. It smelled musty and old. Finally, they came to a door which he unlocked and went into a small office with just one window, which was covered by a large rose bush just now budding out. There was a big wooden desk under the window, a crucifix on the wall and an old gray-metal filing cabinet in a corner. What a perfect room for a private discussion, Ellen thought. Again she wondered how many anxious and sad mothers the good priest had consoled in that room in this out-of-the-way space with pleasant light and a rose bush, to boot.

"How can I be of service?" Father Louie asked.

"Lupita, who I knew as a girl, told me Hector Hernandez and his family was parishioners of yours. I think you know he was recently found murdered. Actually, I found his body," Ellen said, with tears in her eyes.

"Oh, yes, Hector," the priest bowed his head slightly, and he seemed to be sad and contemplative. "Yes, I know about his death. But I did not know you had a connection, Ellen. Information travels fast in our little community here on the west side. I was so sorry to hear about his demise and in such a brutal fashion. I knew him mostly as a boy, a kind and considerate one.

He was an altar boy here for awhile. I know he helped his late mother Maria. He came from one of the families I see so much here – dad in jail, girls married early, boys get into gangs and often then to jail. It seems to be a plight of these people. They work so hard, mostly in restaurants, landscaping companies and construction. But life is always so hard. I am afraid the church has not helped them much with our doctrine on non-birth control."

"I understand, Father. You know I grew up in Denver and often heard and read in the newspapers about the troubles of the Hispanic people in this community. Life here on the west side was so different than where I grew up in southeast Denver. Our dads had jobs and our moms were involved in the community, the school and church. My own mom was a member of our church's Altar and Rosary Society. We were expected to go to school and to do well. But as you know, Father, it was not perfect. In our neighborhoods with their manicured lawns and pink petunias blooming in flagstone planters, there was often a great deal of unhappiness caused by 'keeping up with the Jones,' striving for power and prestige. Alcohol – and I would dare say post trauma stress disorder of fathers who served in WW II or Korea – fueled much of the abuse, which was never reported or talked about. Where did you come from, Father Louie?"

"I was born in the Midwest to parents with German heritage. I was called to the priesthood and eventually to this parish twenty years or so ago. I had to learn Spanish. It wasn't easy. I had to gain the trust of these Hispanic people, who are my flock in the Church's terminology. For awhile, I taught in one of the nearby Catholic schools, but it closed like so many of them. What a shame. I think education would help break the plague of poverty this community suffers from. I don't know how long our little church will stay open. Frankly, I suspect in the next five to ten years it will close, and I will retire then," he concluded.

"I'm sure you have seen and heard a lot and often felt helpless," Ellen said.

"Yes," Father Louie agreed and added, "I know you have too, Ellen, as a member of Al-Anon. I know it is referred to as a 'we program' and listening to other members is an integral part of helping one another."

Ellen closed her eyes and nodded.

"So, Father, I know this might sound crazy, but my cousin and I are trying to help the police find the murderer because of a very worldly and ulterior motive. We are planning a Pink Blossoms Garden and Neighborhood Tour in honor of Mamie Eisenhower in my neighborhood. The proceeds will benefit our local schools. You know where I live now there are many pink crabapple trees, which were planted in honor of the former First Lady who grew up in Denver. With the surge of interest in mid-century modern homes like mine, people are very interested in learning more about them and this special time in our history. The police force is working on the case, but they have so much to do, you know. So my cousin and I are doing as much research as we can to help them. We so hope the murder is solved before the tour and we so hope the blossoms don't freeze if we have snow. That is why I am here today. What can you tell me about Hector? We already know he worked at Lupita's with his mom and for a while after her death. He continued to live in his mom's apartment after her death, but only for a short time. My cousin, who has a real estate associate in this neighborhood, told us some of his friends said Hector was working with a drug guy named Jesus."

The priest seemed to stiffen at that name.

"You know Jesus, Father?" Ellen asked.

"Yes, I do. He's a clever man, probably one who would have gotten out of this community with a high school degree and maybe a little college. I know he is in jail, along with many who worked for him. I know of the anguish his actions caused his family and those families of his workers. But frankly, Ellen, Hector just doesn't seem to fit into that gang," the priest concluded.

"Well, my cousin and I learned Hector at some point got some bookkeeping education, and we're thinking he might have kept Jesus' books and managed inventory, so to speak. We're curious if you might know where Hector was living after his mother's death."

"I never saw Hector again after Maria's funeral. So I don't know where he was living. But what you said seems logical to me. Location of where he was living? Mmmm? There are lots of old dilapidated buildings in this neighborhood. Some of them were old stores, small businesses, and even an old school and some churches. I don't know how many there are. There's that old warehouse area, too, which is not far from here. I wish I knew if one of them was where Jesus had his operations. You might start – as they say on television – pardon me – 'casing out some of these joints.' It seems to me it would have to be heated with something – maybe check with the utility company or maybe they just used space heaters. Also, I think Hector would have needed water and a sewer. That's my suggestion. Sorry I could not be of more help. I am only 'thinking out loud,' as they say."

"I do have a question for you, Ellen."

"Yes, Father."

"Do you know when they will be releasing the

125

body? I'd like to give him a decent burial."

"When I hear, Father, I will let you know. Thank you so much for your time."

As the priest and Ellen were shaking hands, she asked, "By the way, Father, the rose bush outside of your window. Do you know the name?"

"Yes, Ellen, believe it or not, it is a white rose named 'Pope John!'"

Ellen smiled and Father Louie led them through the basement maze, up the stairs and then out the door.

I bet you Father Louie might be right, Ellen thought. Jesus' operation may be located in one of those old buildings. Seems like Betty Nobel recently told me her architectural firm is working on an historical preservation application for that old warehouse area. I bet they have a good idea of which ones are now vacant. I'll give her a call and ask her to send me any information she has.

Before heading south on Santa Fe Drive, Ellen drove to the old warehouse area. She thought, boy, it is creepy. Most of the windows are broken, and there are weeds all over. I remember crawling through an old warehouse with a group of preservationists. There was pigeon poop all over! Wait till Murph hears about this!

CHAPTER FIFTEEN
SONS
... HE BOASTED A LOT ABOUT PARTYING, DRINKING AND DRUGGING ...

Ellen turned down the cement alley and hit her garage door opener. Just before she was going to pull into her garage, she saw Sam and his wife Nancy and Dungaree. Sam motioned to her to join them. She pulled into the garage, turned off the car, got out of her Honda and walked over to the group.

"Oh, hi, Ellen," Nancy greeted her. Have you met Inspector Dungaree?"

"Yep. In this very alley. He rescued me from Brent one day," Ellen's eyes twinkled as she shyly looked at the cop and smiled.

"Well, we saw him snooping around your garage, Ellen, so we came out here to see who was casing your joint, so to speak," with twinkling blue eyes Sam chortled as much as his artificial voice box would permit.

Ellen laughed and when she looked at Dungaree a soft red color crept into his cheeks.

"We got to talking, and it seemed like we were all thinking the same thing," Nancy said.

"The same thing?"

"Yeah. The dead guy must have been killed close to your garage, Ellen, because none of us, including the cops, found any blood on the dirt. You know, blows to the head like that guy got cause severe bleeding right away. Also, to the best of Sam's knowledge and mine, the lopper was never found, and the tree pole must not have had any fingerprints on it. If it had, we probably wouldn't be standing here talking about the murder!"

"That is interesting, Nancy. Sounds like the victim got his lights knocked out, so to speak, and then the killer draped him over my chain, mutilated the body and then disappeared somehow with the loppers."

Ellen looked at the three of them and then exclaimed, "We know the cops checked out Axle's equipment, and Axle has not been charged in the murder! Who else around here has that equipment and a motive to kill?"

"Other than Axle, we don't know," Sam said.

He continued, "We were just going over with Dungaree here a possible timeline for the murder."

Dungaree piped in, "I asked them what they could tell me about the morning of the murder."

Nancy said, "I remember Sam and I got home a little early and did not have to put up with Axle blocking the alley. So it was before 7 a.m. I think Ellen pulls out of her garage around 6:45 for her yoga class."

Dungaree asked, "Did the rest of your neighbors' houses seem any different that morning?"

"Well, let me think," Nancy contemplated. "Annie's house was the same. I don't think she gets up that early, and I don't remember seeing any lights on. It was Wednesday, and Ellen had her yellow chain up. It's hard to see in her yard – impossible, really – because of her new fence. Axle's lights were on. I'm not sure if the woman he has been living with was there or not. She left – or tries to leave him – quite frequently because he is so degrading. I don't know if he is physically abusive or not. I just know Axle can be very threatening and intimidating. Brent and Joan's lights were on as usual. Brent is abusive, too. His first wife left him because of it. I know he was court ordered to take anger management classes. I don't know if they helped or not. He's been remarried for about seven years now. His new wife, Joan, is not as quiet as the woman who lives with Axle, but her eyes tell me a lot. I feel sorry for their two little girls. They are ages six and four I think. Brent is a strong man and drinks a lot. Keith told me Brent's son had a drinking problem, too. You know he was in a car accident not too long ago, right Inspector?"

"Yes, I do know."

"So do Brent and his wife work?" Dungaree asked.

Nancy said, "She's an administrative assistant for Lavoy Company, and Brent works at Fort Logan as a guard and maybe does some maintenance work, too. He works the morning shift."

"What time does he go to work?" Dungaree inquired.

"Well, we don't really know," Sam stated. "We leave before he does and get home after he has left. I never see his wife's car in the garage. She must park it on the street."

Ellen said, "I haven't met Brent's current wife. I understand she agreed to set up a fudge stand for us at the tour. Brent seems to have a lot of rage. You know, Nancy and Sam, he threatened me when Buttercup and I were in the alley. I was trying to get in touch with Joan and wanted to ask him when I might reach her. Instead, he came after Buttercup and me. Fortunately, Dungaree entered the alley about that time, saw what was happening, and rescued us. Where is his first wife now? I feel so sorry for her because she lost her son, and he was responsible for the deaths of other teenagers because of the alcohol and drugs in his system that awful night."

Ellen noticed Dungaree winced when she mentioned the cause of the deaths. Maybe cops really never do get over these senseless deaths, she mused.

Nancy said, "Lavonne Broderick lost year her

16-year-old son, whose name was Todd. You know, boys of this age can be so cruel to their mothers. Thank goodness, Keith treats me well. Lavonne is the head nurse of surgery at St. Anthony's North. It is a large hospital and a Level 1 Trauma Center. I think it has been the community for over 100 years. Lavonne has a good job, an important job, a job that pays well. She still has dark hair and is very attractive woman."

She paused, took a deep breath and then continued, "One day I saw Lavonne in the alley after she divorced Brent. She told me her relationship with Todd was awful: he was belligerent, and she had no control over him. His grades had dropped dramatically. Lavonne told me Todd never hit her like his father did when she was married to him, but he was just as mean. She said Todd drank all the time. Lavonne suspected her son was an alcoholic like his father. He spent more and more time with his dad even though this was against the court order. Brent told Lavonne he gave Todd a car because she worked such long hours and could not take her son where he needed to go. Lavonne started sobbing and walked away. I never saw her again. They did not have a funeral for their son."

Ellen's eyes filled with tears, and she lowered her head. When she looked up, Nancy and Sam's son was coming down the alley. He joined the group and gave his mom a hug.

Sam introduced Keith to Dungaree and explained why they were all in the alley.

Dungaree asked, "Son, what can you tell me about the morning of the murder? I understand that you departed for school after your parents left for work. Did you hear or see anything unusual?"

Keith squirmed a little and said, "No, sir. I got up a little late that day and was dashing to get ready for school before mom and dad got back. I was in the shower, had the TV on and gobbled my breakfast. I'm afraid I can't be of any help to you."

"I understand," Dungaree stated, "but maybe you can help me a little regarding   I'm sorry to bring him up, your childhood friend Todd."

Keith grew a little red in the face, not expecting this question. He thought he was off the hook because he had not heard or seen anything. "I remember playing with him when we were little kids before he moved away."

"Well, what about his reputation in high school – was he a jock, nerd or what?"

Keith's face reddened at this question. "Well, sir, I did not have much to do with him. He was in one of my classes if he came to school at all. Todd certainly was not a jock or a nerd. He boasted a lot about partying, drinking and drugging."

"Listen, son, I know this is hard for you and maybe particularly hard with your parents and Ellen here. As a cop, because you are under 18, I have to have one of your parents here to ask you questions; but I can tell you, every generation – my generation, your mother and father's and winking at Ellen, maybe your neighbor's, have had classmates that partied a lot. Maybe in some generations drugs were not so prevalent. But I know from personal experience and as a cop drugs are part of the deal now along with the alcohol."

Dungaree's words seemed to help Keith a little. He bowed his head and then raised his eyes and said, "Yes, sir. Todd was a big partier."

"Any idea where he got the booze and marijuana or whatever?"

Keith answered, "Kids, like my former neighbor, often get some help from their parents."

"Yeah, not uncommon. Did you ever hear Todd like boast where he got his supply?"

"Well, one time, I did hear him say 'thanks to my dad.'" Nancy gasped.

"Yes," Dungaree said. "I was wondering about that. Did Todd have a girl friend?"

"Yes, sir, she died with him along with his best friend and his girl friend," Keith hung his head and Dungaree knew not to press him.

"That took a lot of guts, Keith. Thank you. I would imagine this is not easy for your parents to hear," Dungaree looked at them and Ellen, too. They all had tears in their eyes.

Nancy put her arm around Keith, and Sam put his arm around Nancy. The family turned quietly towards their backyard and started to walk home.

Ellen looked at Dungaree. She saw some tears in his eyes, too. "It looks like this isn't easy for you to hear, either."

"It never is. Even after all these years."

They heard a small dog yapping and turned around. Candy seemed to be skipping towards them because her little dog was pulling so hard on her leash. "My, my, my. We meet again in this funny little alley. I am sorry, Officer, I forgot your name."

"Dungaree, ma'am. I was just getting ready to leave. Goodbye, ladies." Dungaree turned around, walked past Ellen's garage and then went up the cement alley to get to his car.

"Ellen, I have great news for you! The Pink Poodles and Bangs Brigade has come up with the perfect solution for our dogs!"

Oh, boy, Ellen thought. Now what? I have just listened to some gut wrenching information about Brent and his son, and this scatter-brained woman now wants to tell me about dyeing dogs pink! She tried her

132

best to remain calm and to smile a little. All those morning yoga classes seemed to help now because she heard her teacher tell the class to soften their faces.

She said to Candy, "That's exciting. What did you women come up with? "

"I don't know if you know this, Ellen, but we all love to knit. One of the nurses came across this easy and darling coat we can make for our dogs. So each of us has been knitting and they are almost done!"

"Oh, this is great news, Candy! What a wonderful solution now the world is more conscious about animals. I love it."

"Well, I am glad, Ellen. I don't know if you heard this today, but we might be getting a blizzard in a day or two. Our dogs will be warm no matter what!"

"No. I had not heard that, Candy. I'm going to go watch the news now. I'll be in touch."

Ellen went in her house, but did not immediately turn on her television. First she let Buttercup outside and then picked up Sweetie Pie and gave her a hug. She let Buttercup back in and then turned on her computer and found the email from Betty Nobel with a pdf attachment. It was a map of all the buildings in the old warehouse area, with certain buildings marked as still in use. Betty explained the utility information was provided to the preservation group along with all of the owners' names and contact information.

Next she grabbed her phone and called her cousin. "Murph, I think it would be best if you spent the night here tomorrow night."

"Why, honey, are you starting to have nightmares? I know after a traumatic event like what you went through - the horror of it all - can often come back to you days, or weeks or even months later."

"Thankfully, I am not. But, I do need to embark on a very scary adventure. I want you to come along. It involves going to the old warehouse district early in the morning and checking out some old buildings. Your sexy little red car will just draw attention to us. My Honda will be less conspicuous, but we will still have to park it outside the district and walk. We don't want anyone to get suspicious. Because we have to leave so early, I think it is best if you spend the night. I just saw Candy in the alley, and she told me a storm is coming, to boot. We'll have to bundle up and wear good boots. Why don't you come over for coffee tomorrow morn and I will fill you in? You can decide then if you want to do this with me or not. I've had quite a day, or I would tell you all about it now."

"Oh, Hon, of course, I will go with you. I'm in this all the way with you. I'll bring some donuts. They always help, you know."

"They sure do, particularly if they are double chocolate!"

Little did Ellen know Dungaree too would be eating chocolate donuts and discussing a similar quest with McCoy and Green in the morning.

CHAPTER SIXTEEN
THE WAREHOUSE
... *WINTER RETURNED TO THE CITY* ...

"Hello, Dungaree," McCoy cheerfully said as he entered the older man's office, carrying a box of chocolate donuts. Dungaree grunted. "I have a special little project for you, one that involves your love for history and architecture and may bring us to the end of the horrible murder in the alley. Doesn't it sound like fun, Dungaree?"

"Oh, kind sir, what horrible deed do you want me to do? It must be dreadful since you are bribing me with chocolate donuts!"

"As you know, we don't know where the victim had been living since his dear mother departed this earth several years ago, nor do we know how he fed himself after he quit the restaurant where he and his mother worked."

"What a wee bit of knowledge to base this request for me to do a special project."

Chuckling, McCoy went on, "Further, I think the victim worked for the drug lord Jesus Mendoza, but not in the usual sense. I'm thinking he managed the books and ordered and controlled inventory. And I got a call from Ellen." He winked at Dungaree. McCoy guessed he had some admiration for this intelligent older woman since Dungaree seemed to perk up whenever her name was mentioned. "Ellen told me about a conversation she had today with a priest. Father Louie knew Hector Hernandez since he was a young boy. And, get this -- this good man of the cloth suggested Hector lived in Mendoza's old office and warehouse. Father Louie told her the location may be in one of the vacant buildings on the west side, and I believe you have an understanding of that real estate."

"So what you are asking me to do is to go crawl around these putrid, rat-infested supposedly abandoned buildings to find the corporate headquarters of Mendoza Drugs and the CEO's former office and his chief financial officer's private condo? You got to be kidding me. I have eighty-six days – repeat, eighty-six days before I retire, McCoy! I'm not going to go looking for rat holes!"

McCoy knew Dungaree was serious because his gray eyes looked like steel bolts, holding together the wrinkles on the older man's face.

"Now, would I put you in such a spot?" McCoy asked with a slight grin on his face.

"Don't go sweet talking me, McCoy!"

Well actually, I am trying to make it as easy as possible for you. I have already sent orders to get the utility and water bills for many of these derelict properties. Ellen is sending me a list she got from the architect, working with her on the Pink Blossoms tour, and whose firm is writing the application to the National Trust for Historic Preservation. The list has the names of the buildings' owners. I did not know the area is being considered for historic designation. Maybe you did, Dungaree?"

"So you're putting our officers – the lifeblood of our police department at risk, McCoy?" Dungaree snapped.

"Well, actually, you know as well as I do that's part of police work."

"What specifically am I looking for, McCoy? I can go myself without putting one of our officers, who probably has a family, at risk."

"First of all, find someplace you think someone is living or who has recently lived in. Second, check the place out. See if there are computers we can crash or supply we can confiscate. Third, look for any books or files or anything that might have names and info listed. Not everyone uses computers or sometimes they have backup systems. Fourth, fingerprints or any prints will be helpful. Don't do this alone, Dungaree. Do you read me?"

"Yes," Dungaree reluctantly agreed. "And if we find said corporate suites what do you want me to do?"

"Call for discrete backups and me ASAP," McCoy said.

"So you have this list for me?"

"It should be in my office. I will get it to you right away. I'm thinking Jesus was a big enough dude he and Hector weren't peeing in cans or making a campfire to keep warm. Who knows, there might even be a refrigerator with goodies in it and a stove and maybe even a shower."

"Alright, alright. But I expect some special compensation from you, McCoy, when I find this luxury townhouse."

"You got it, Dungaree. Lynn and I will have you over for home cooked meals for a month!"

"Thanks, McCoy."

After McCoy left his office, Dungaree closed his door, went back to his desk and sat down. A huge sigh escaped his body. He did not want to go in this area where so many desperate people had died. Drugs and booze and gambling, oh and lust, seemed to be the driving force of all men who went down the wrong path, ending at the graveyard or jail in many cases. He thought of his own drinking days and the hell he put his family through. Booze had seemed the only way he could cope with this job, with life. It had been the bane of his father and his father before him. A little golden swig gave a man such courage, such self-esteem, such bravado. It had worked for a long time. He had solved a number of really tough cases by his booze-induced lack of fear. He had confronted many desperados. He had shouted them down. Gunned them down in a few cases.

But then the golden remedy quit working. He needed more and more of it just to get to work each day. He hated himself. He knew his family knew, and he knew it wouldn't be long before the department learned his courage secret. He tried to quit, but he couldn't. He didn't know what to do. One day he wandered into just such a stinking warehouse hole as McCoy just suggested. He walked in and found four men near death from alcohol, and later he learned, from shooting up heroin, too. He called for backup. Ambulances came. The men were taken to the general hospital where they died after some heroic efforts to save them, costing the tax payers thousands and thousands of dollars.

Dungaree was scared. He knew that would be his fate too, if he didn't get help. That day he went into his boss' office and told him his deepest, darkest secret. Thank God he understood. Thank God his boss arranged assistance for him. He took a leave of absence and went to a rehab hospital. He started attending Alcoholics Anonymous meetings there and never quit.

Every morning at 6 a.m. he went to a large old home near downtown Denver where meetings were held. He went to the second floor and entered a big room. Every seat was taken by men and women, who by the grace of God were sober that day.

Dungaree became a more cautious cop and a more compassionate one. He knew first-hand about the cunning of this disease. Each morning he thanked the God of his understanding for another day and a chance to help someone else who had been on the path of annihilation. And now he was helping McCoy with the investigation into the death of Hernandez, the man brutally killed in the alley. He wondered if the 16-year-old boy he heard about from the neighbors yesterday was somehow connected to all of this.

There was a knock on his door. He opened it and a pretty, young administrative assistant said, "Here is the information from McCoy, sir."

"Why, thank you," Dungaree said kindly and then closed his door.

Yes, indeed! Dungaree thought. Here are the utility and water bills from all those deserted old warehouses down by the railroad tracks. Life had changed since these old buildings were constructed 100-years or so ago. They had been full of machinery and all sorts of goods from suitcases to grain. Shipping them via rail was easy. Now, many of those businesses had closed their doors or built new facilities out east. Goods were no longer shipped by rail. They left the Mile High City via truck or plane. Dungaree called Green. He was grooming him to take over his job and to fine hone his investigative skills. Green was in the building and came immediately to his office.

"What ya got, Dungaree?" he asked.

"These are utility company bills for the old warehouse district on the west side. Many of these buildings have not had any service for years. You know those places where we find drunk bums sitting around a fire in a big can or a fire they made from wood in the building. But a few still do have electric and gas service. We need to find those who are current customers of the utility company. Maybe some or even just one hasn't paid their bill lately because the bookkeeper got atrociously murdered recently, and the landlord is in jail."

139

"So then what do we do, go collect for the utility company?"

"Hardly, son. We stealthily break in – following department procedures, of course – and then see what we find like may be some dope, computers, files, and guns, etc. You know the usual." Green nodded.

Dungaree handed him half the stack. "Go through these, Green, and see if you come up with any active ones. I'll go through the rest."

Green pulled his chair close to a side table, turned on a lamp and started looking through the bills.

Two hours later, each man had pulled out a small stack of active accounts. "Good," said Dungaree. "Why don't you take a break? I am going up to McCoy's area and see if they have a stack of water and sewer bills for us to leaf through. The guys we are looking for are high-class dudes. As McCoy said, he doubted they were peeing into cans." Green's eyes opened wide. "Come back in a half-hour or so, and we'll do this again."

Dungaree shuffled out of his office and locked the door behind him. He took the elevator up two floors to McCoy's office. The pretty assistant was on the phone. She professionally completed her call and said, "Can I help you, Officer Dungaree?"

"Well, yes, ma'am," he said, blushing a little. "McCoy said you might have another stack of bills for me to pay – he winked – from the water and sewer company."

"Oh, yes, sir." She got up out of her chair and went to a filing cabinet where she pulled out a thick envelope and handed it to him. "Hope you have lots of money in your checking account, sir," she said, winking back at him.

A wink from a pretty lady, oh, such a simple joy, Dungaree thought as he walked to the elevator.

Green was waiting for him outside his door. "Come in, my good sir," Dungaree said. Once again, he divided the pile and the two men bent their heads down over the bills. A couple of hours later each had a stack.

"Now what?" asked the younger cop.

"That's an easy question to answer, Green. What do you think we should do next, given what I told you?"

"Match them. See if any have electricity, water and sewer, sir."

"Yep," Dungaree purred.

Close to 5 p.m. each man had a small pile of active bills. Dungaree looked up at the clock, and chuckling, said, "Cocktail time, my boy. Time to go home. Come back in the morning. But before you leave the house, play with your dog a few extra minutes."

Green gulped. He knew he and Dungaree would be calling on these "respectful" businesses. He wasn't sure why he became a cop. Risk and fear were part of the job.

Winter returned to the city the next morning. It was cold and blustery and there were four inches of snow or more on the ground.

Dungaree had a fresh pot of coffee waiting for Green when he arrived in his office. "Well, good morning, Green," Dungaree cheerfully said. "Fine weather for Canadian geese, I must say. And fine weather for finding criminals – we might be lucky to find footprints in the snow. Every cop's dream. Right, Green?" The younger man grunted.

"Let's see what matches we have here," Dungaree said as he handed Green his stack.

After a while and a couple of gulps of coffee, Green said, "Well, sir, I only have three here."

"Well, that's just fine. I have three, too. Let's hit

the road, Green. I don't know if footprints in the snow will be our clue or not. It's my understanding the last inhabitant of the corporate suite we are looking for is now in the morgue. But who knows, maybe someone else has already moved in," Dungaree said as he put on his coat, stocking hat and a hand-knitted muffler.

A half hour later the cops were in the old warehouse area of several blocks of old buildings. Many of the windows were broken. Hundreds of pigeons huddled under the eaves, protecting themselves from the sudden change in weather. Numerous cigarette butts, covered with snow, were on the sidewalk.

The wind blew and the car's defroster labored under the cold weather. The addresses were within a few blocks of each other. However, each building had been subdivided years ago, so it would be necessary for the cops at times to get out of their vehicle and walk on the broken, icy sidewalks, piles of rubbish or railroad tracks to find the specific company.

"How should we go about this, sir? Should we just put them in street order, look for tracks or life or no tracks at all?" Green asked his superior.

"Excellent question, Green! I don't really know the answer. I don't want us to be obvious out here because I know there are lots of homeless people in these abandoned ruins, and they have a way of communicating with each other. On the other hand, I don't like to be cold in my old age so a logical numeric search appeals to me. That way we don't have to back track or crisscross," Dungaree pondered. "Oh, hell, let's do it numerically. Got your gun ready, just in case, Green?"

"Yes, sir."

Dungaree parked the car several blocks away, put his police phone in his pocket and made sure his pistol was on his hip. "Let's go. Watch your step,"

Dungaree said as he hopped out of the car and locked it.

The wind whipped Dungaree's muffler across his face and his glasses fogged up. They got to the first address. The sign on the door said XYZ Company, makers of fine leather goods. The cops could see an old man sitting at a sewing machine, so they moved on to the next address, which was in the next building, just around the corner. There, they found what appeared to be an active business with its hours posted on the door. They were not due to open for a couple more hours.

Then, Dungaree and Green had a two-block walk between several buildings. The wind and snow swirled around the corners, and Dungaree prayed they did not find a dead drunk curled up next to one of the buildings or a dog or cat for that matter. At one point, Green tripped on several old bottles but quickly regained his footing.

It hardly seemed worth the walk because when they got to the next establishment there was a sign on the door which said, "If snowy and blowy tomorrow, we won't be open." Fortunately, the next address was a short walk away. Dungaree saw a drunk bum passed out in a doorway and nudged him with his shoe when he walked by. The man groaned and tuned over. Bastard will probably be okay and not freeze, Dungaree told himself.

At the fourth address, none of the lights were on. The cops peeked through the dirty windows and could see an old desk in the corner and heard a phone ring. They decided to move on, thinking the business owner did not bother to come in on such a blustery day. At the fifth establishment they saw a woman bustling around, barking orders to a couple of men, "I don't give a hoot if it's snowing. Get these boxes and get out the door and get them delivered!" she ordered the men. Dungaree and Green scurried on.

They had a block to walk in an open area. The snow was increasing and the wind blew it either sideways or in big swooping swirls. Damn, thought Dungaree, eighty-five days!

At the next building, there were footprints leading up to the entrance. They looked like they had been made by fairly new boots in a small size. The door was slightly ajar. Dungaree caught Green's gaze and signaled to put his hand on the gun. Dungaree boldly walked in and shouted, "Police." Something moved in a dimly lit corner, and Green pointed his gun at it.

A soft female voice whispered, "Officer Green." He could not believe he recognized the voice. It was Mary Mahoncy. "I believe this man is near death."

Another female voice whispered, "Inspector Dungaree, the door was open, and we heard someone groaning. We peered in the window and saw this man wriggling in pain. We came in because the man obviously needed help right away. To get to him, we had to walk past this old desk. I looked down at the desk and found this handwritten list. My cousin and I hid the best we could when we heard you coming. We didn't know who you were and feared you might be the killer. That's why we did not come forward when you came through the door. Thank goodness it was you because I think me and my cousin have found Jesus Mendoza's old office and on this desk, believe it or not, is a list of his clients. I knew not to touch it."

Dungaree pointed his phone's flashlight at Ellen. The beam revealed a pair of lovely hazel green eyes.

The man on the floor moaned as best he could, "Don't shoot!"

144

Green hurried over to Murph with his gun pointed at the man, who might have a gun or knife on him and still have energy to use it.

Dungaree strode over to Ellen. "My dear woman, what are you ladies doing here? This is a very dangerous situation."

"We thought we would find this office and information leading to the murderer after I talked with Father Louie yesterday. It made sense to us because it is so run down and isolated. When we were kids, this area had many vibrant businesses. Denver grew and most of the businesses left, but the train still runs through. That would be so helpful for Mendoza's drug deliveries. Dungaree, I looked through the names and was aghast the last name on it is Brent Broderick!"

"Oh, I wish you had told me you were coming here this morning. I would have told you not to come. You and your cousin are in a very perilous place and now an active police situation. I am going to call for our backup team and McCoy now. Thank you for letting me know about the list and why you came into the building. Our officers will escort you and your cousin to your car after they arrive. For now, I would like you and your cousin to get on the opposite wall from this man. We don't know what condition he is in. He may have a weapon on him and garner the energy to use it. Please don't touch anything. Green, keep your gun out."

After Dungaree called for backups and McCoy, he went over to the man. His breath reeked of alcohol and his whole body oozed urine. "Who are you? Do you work here?" he commanded. The man didn't answer. "Okay, sir, you are under arrest for possibly trespassing if you are not connected to this business and avoiding an officer. Green, book him!" At that, the man got up on all fours and the officers could see he was very, very drunk. "Green, call the detox unit and babysit this guy while I look around."

"Yes, sir," said Green.

Dungaree turned on the lights. The room was amazingly in good order despite the fact this guy and maybe others had broken in. There were a couple of desks, their drawers open, but the contents not disturbed. A small laptop was stashed in one of them. Along the sides was some shelving. They were empty, but Dungaree detected a faint white substance on some of them. He called McCoy. "Think you want to come down here, McCoy, and look at some interesting items. We have an inebriated individual in here. Detox is on their way. And, sir, Ellen Lane and her cousin are here. Seems they were trying to find Mendoza's operation, too."

Two burley officers with the detox unit showed up in the door. Dungaree said, "Please take John Doe in, but first let me read him his rights since he is under arrest for presumably breaking and entering."

He read the man his rights and silently hoped the guy wouldn't die in route to the general hospital's detox unit. He also hoped, and said a little prayer, too, the guy would admit his problem and get on the road to recovery. "Oh, and while you are at it, there is another one who needs to go to detox before he freezes to death," Dungaree stated, giving the officers directions where to find the person in this warehouse area.

The drunk was lifted onto a stretcher and transported to the detox van outside.

"Ladies, officers will be here shortly to safely escort you to your car."

McCoy walked in and whistled. "Wow, just like the priest suggested we find."

"Well, don't bank on it, McCoy. You'll want to

pay special attention to the written note Ms. Lane found on the desk." He nodded to Ellen. "Particularly the last name on the list, her neighbor Mr. Broderick. Will do fingerprints and then bring the computer and files back to our office. You need to alert whoever is paying the utility bills about our police activity."

"Well, seems like they are in arrears. Jesus Mendoza, the name of the account, is in jail." McCoy stated.

Other officers arrived and two of them came up to Ellen and Murph. McCoy stated, "Ellen, these men will now escort you to your car. We will take it from here. You have been very helpful to us. But I need to ask you to let us do our work now. If you have any more concerns or ideas, please contact me immediately."

CHAPTER SEVENTEEN
THE COMPANY
…MAINLY SMALL FIRES STARTED BY DESPERATE PEOPLE SEEKING WARMTH…

After Ellen and her cousin got back to Ellen's house, she made a cup of hot chocolate for both of them. "Geez, that was spooky. So it seems Brent is a customer, so to speak, of Hector's. But it doesn't make any sense he would kill his supplier. Does it, Murph?" Ellen asked.

Wrapping her hands around the warm cup, Murph took a sip of the chocolate before responding. "I don't know. He seems to be such a weird and angry guy from the way he treats his wife and the way he came after you in the alley the day you were trying to connect with her about the fudge sale."

"Yes. He sure seems bizarre and mad to me, too. I'm thinking he might have been the guy I saw with the gun pointed at the tree the first Thanksgiving Day I lived here. How awful he was supplying his son with booze and drugs. As a Bosnian vet, I suspect he has PTSD and uses drugs and booze to numb his pain. But I don't understand why he would get stuff for his son, and it makes no sense to me he would kill his supplier, if Hector was his supplier."

The cousins sat in silence and watched the snow fall on Ellen's crabapple tree outside her window. "Oh, geez! Look at it snow. I wonder if the blossoms will freeze. Let's check the weather forecast. Then we'd better get back to the committee about the tour. Hopefully, the blossoms won't die, and we can put a reassuring note on our web site." When her cat, Sweetie Pie, jumped on her lap, she jerked and spilt some chocolate. "I guess I am a little jumpy after what we went through this morning!"

***

Back at the office, McCoy did contact the utility companies and told them the property in question is under police investigation, and furthermore the responsible person on the account had been in jail for some time. He did not know who had actually paid the account. The companies were asked to continue their services for several more days until the police investigation was complete.

Next, he searched the list Ellen sent him for the name of the owner of the building. It turned out the building is owned by a large out-of-state railroad conglomerate, with a city property management company. McCoy called the company, and after spending minutes in the company's "phone tree," finally reached a live person named Doris. He identified himself and said he would like to speak with the manager.

Doris said he is not in, but he could leave a message in his voice mail box.

"Before I do, I want you to know this property is under active police investigation, and we suspect it is connected in some way to a brutal murder that recently occurred. Doris, I need for you to get in touch with this manager – what is his name? – because I need to interview him right away." He felt Doris was not in a very cooperative mood, so he added, "Or we will have to subpoena him and everyone in the office."

With this last statement, Doris's mood seemed to change and she said, "I will get in touch with Mr. Bautch right away, sir."

Within minutes, just long enough for McCoy to get a warm cup of coffee, Bautch called him back.

"What's this about?"

"I would be upset too if I had gotten a call from a cop demanding to see me. Let's say this is part of a murder investigation. I would like to come to your office in the Denver Tech Center to talk with you and fill you in on what's happening. Would right after lunch, say 1 p.m., today work?" McCoy said.

Bautch angrily replied, "I'll make it work. See you at 1!"

McCoy headed south and east to the sprawling Denver Tech Center and then pulled into one of the shopping centers at its fringe. He went into a Whole Foods store that had a spacious cafeteria in the center of the store. He wanted some good food and to think. He did not want anyone to identify him. He parked his car fairly close to the building. The blustery weather had kept many shoppers at home. He walked through the opening front doors and felt immediately warm air being pushed down on the entrance point. The displays in the food court showcased fresh oranges and asparagus. Oh, I love asparagus. Maybe Lynn and I can cook some this weekend, McCoy thought.

He headed to the food court and bought a plate of rigatoni with marinara sauce on it, a small salad, and a cup of hot coffee. He put the pasta and coffee down on a small table near the edge of the court and went back and got a salad, arugula, chopped egg, mushrooms, carrot, and little tomatoes. Compared to what he ate most days for lunch, this was a feast.

Sitting down, McCoy took a deep breath and started gathering his thoughts. He was fairly confident Jesus and Hector's office had been found along with computer files and other information that would support their operation. The film of white powder on the shelves would probably turn out to be heroin and/or other drugs. Since nothing was left on those shelves, he thought either street people or gangs had come in and cleaned out the supply. He needed to have a valid reason why the cops went into Bautch's space. He wondered if Bautch is connected to the business. McCoy suspected Hector was selling dope to Brent Broderick and knew Broderick supplied his son with some of it and certainly, liquor.

He ate a couple of forkfuls of pasta and then some of his salad.

What would be his approach to Bautch? First, to show legitimacy in going into the office space. Dungaree told him the door was ajar, and saw a man curled up in a corner. He could – if need be – use this information to explain why Dungaree and Green were in the area. Second, he wanted to know how Bautch was collecting rent and from whom.

McCoy finished his lunch, hit the john, and hurried back to his car. The wind was still blustery and more snow was coming down.

He turned into the large business center and then pulled into a parking lot of gargantuan steel and glass building. The name of the railroad company printed in 6-foot letters hung just below the roof. Probably the company managed many of the railroad conglomerate's assets. He parked close to the entrance and entered one of the large doors. It must have been 20-feet high itself. Inside there were huge pots of blooming spring flowers and a guard's desk.

A burley man barked at him, "Who are you here to see, sir?"

McCoy responded, "Mr. Bautch."

The guard asked if he had an appointment, and McCoy stated with no anger or malice in his voice (a skill he had practiced for years),"He is expecting me." The guard made a phone call and a short time later a nearby elevator door opened and a shapely young woman with long blond hair came out of it and strode up to McCoy.

"Officer McCoy, right this way," she said without introducing herself. McCoy followed her and watched the guard's jaw drop.

She did not say one word to him as they rode the elevator to the top twenty-second floor. When the door opened McCoy found himself in one of the most expensively decorated rooms he had ever been in. The wood floors were the real thing, the carpets – oriental – expensive, the artwork was original, the plants were huge and green and the furniture looked like it was handcrafted. A man came forward with an expensive, exquisitely tailored gray Armani suit. He extended his hand, "Officer McCoy, I am Mr. Bautch." He led the man to his office door and said, "Thanks, Doris."

"Okay, McCoy, what is this all about?" Bautch said edgily.

"So, I understand your company is the property manager for a large warehouse building, built in 1902, and used for many years by a paper company. The railroad company bought it about 60 years ago, and then divided it into various spaces which they leased to a variety of companies. One by one most of these companies left. Some are still in business today in other locations, and some closed their doors. Now, to the best of our knowledge, only one company remained, which, according the utility companies' records, is owned by Jesus Manzanares. This company occupied the entire first floor. The rest of the building is vacant, except for homeless people, who seek its shelter. This building is one of many in the area. Few companies are located in them, and over the years have seen quite a bit of police activity, mainly small fires started by desperate people seeking warmth and individuals taken to the detox unit at general hospital or to the morgue."

"Yeah, so what, McCoy? What does this have to do with a murder investigation and what were you doing in my building?" Bautch demanded.

"Frankly, Bautch, we were looking for Manzanarez' company."

"Well, duh, couldn't the utility company give you the address?" Bautch said.

"Oh indeed they did, and so did the other utility companies," McCoy said. "When was the last time you saw Jesus Manzanarez, Bautch?"

"Is he dead – murdered?"

"No," said McCoy. "Just wondering when you saw him last."

"Oh, I have never seen Manzanares."

"Do you not have a lease contract form, detailing who you are leasing to?"

Bautch faced reddened. "Not really. If someone wants to lease space in that old building, as long as they pay their rent, we don't investigate them."

"Mmmm," McCoy said. "Did Manzanares pay his rent on time?"

"Always," Bautch stated.

"With a check?" McCoy inquired.

"No, with an automatic withdrawal from a bank account."

"How interesting. May I see the account information?"

"Absolutely not, unless you have a court order!" Bautch stated emphatically.

"Well, that would be a snap to get, Bautch. Manzanarez has been in jail for a number of years," McCoy replied calmly.

"Really," Bautch said as his face whitened.

"Yes, on the tip of an elderly lady, we nabbed

153

him and his drug gang a number of years ago. Jesus is in a state penitentiary, and will likely stay there for most of his life."

"Well, how can that be since we continue to receive rent from him?" Bautch asked.

"I doubt you will receive rent from him next month because I believe there is a good chance we found his bookkeeper, Hector Hernadez, chief financial officer, if you will, and office manager. He was brutally murdered in an alley in Englewood recently. Funny thing is the dead man did not have an address, tax or employment records for a number of years. We suspected he was living in one of these buildings and possibly selling off any inventory Manzanarez had left."

"Well, so what? That is not a reason and you have no legal right to go into my building!" Bautch said confrontationally.

"Actually, sir, the door was open and there was a man on the floor who appeared dead or near-death. As police officers we are bound to enter and to assist," McCoy informed Bautch.

"Really! Who was it?"

"The man was barely alive, we had a unit take him to the detox unit at general hospital, and we charged him with breaking and entering," McCoy informed Bautch. "After we took care of him, we declared this to be a crime scene and by law confiscated computers, files, shelves and drugs."

Bautch turned deadly white and meek. "Neither I nor my company was involved in any of this, McCoy," he said.

"Well, that might be true. My advice to you sir, is to get a lawyer. A court order is on its way to you along with our investigating team. We will want to see all of your records, regarding Manzanarez. The health department is in your building now. My guess is they will condemn it. Further, just for you to know, our police radios are often monitored by the press. I wouldn't be surprised if reporters arrive at your beautiful door soon, wanting to know about your operation and buildings," McCoy said as he rose and walked out of the door.

"Oh, oh," Bautch said out loud and picked up his phone to call the company's legal department.

McCoy got in his car and started to drive home. He had had enough for one day. Then he got a call from Dungaree. "How about you come into my office tomorrow morning for a cup of some of my great coffee?" he said.

"Oh, I would be delighted to," McCoy sarcastically said. "I hope you have information for me worth that rot gut!"

"Now, McCoy, would I bother you if I didn't?" Dungaree stated and ended the call.

His phone rang again. "Captain McCoy, Ellen Lane here. I would like to talk with you tomorrow. I'm feeling really jittery – actually, a little scared. It seems to me Brent is the killer, and he lives almost behind my house."

"I can understand why you would be fearful, Ellen. Yes, I will stop by tomorrow, say around 10:30. For now, I will have an officer near your home."

"Thank you, McCoy. That would be very helpful."

On the way to the office next day, McCoy stopped at Marianne's Bakery and bought a box of cinnamon rolls, the gooey kind with lots of nuts and butter. Arriving at headquarters, he went to his office, told his secretary he was headed to Dungaree's office, and gave her a bunch of the cinnamon rolls for the gang that morning. She suspected it was going to be an eventful and perhaps pivotal meeting, involving this very brutal murder in the alley of those little 1950s homes, so charming and so quintessential to the post-war in cities throughout the region.

McCoy took the elevator, not wanting to spill the rolls. Arriving at Dungaree's door, he put on his most pained look.

Dungaree saw him and gruffly said, "Come in, McCoy. I see you brought me an offering for this fine detective work we have done."

"Actually, sir," McCoy said, "I brought these fine epicurean morsels to conceal the god-awful taste of your coffee!" Then, both men grinned at each other, poured large mugs of coffee, reached for napkins and grabbed gooey buns.

"So?" McCoy said.

"Looks like Hector was a very good company man. He sold all of the product left in Jesus' warehouse, kept the lights on in the building, the bank happy, and a select number of customers content. I think he thought about going into full operation again, but that would mean obtaining new drug supplies and opening up the supply lines again. This would have been very risky for him to do. The inventory dwindled, and most of the bank account went to pay bills. After Hector fell in love, he decided to close the business. He realized he needed a new legitimate job with a potential employer who did not have an employment screening process."

"I see," said McCoy. "Besides the lack of a screening process, why did he join PU Services and Axle Tree Service?"

"Excellent questions, McCoy," Dungaree sarcastically stated and then winked. "You see, his few remaining customers lived along the PU Services route he was assigned to."

"What! You got a list of customers? How did

you do that?"

"Yes, indeed, Officer McCoy. We have a list of his customers, including Brent Broderick."

"Let me see the list!"

"Not so fast, McCoy. First I want to share with you the list of products sold by Jesus. Of course, they included Mexican marijuana and meth, but also cocaine and heroin. We found traces of everything but marijuana on the shelves in the office. Could be Hector himself got a little benefit from these small particles."

"Mmmm. And his last customers were along this route. What would he do? Leave it in their trash cans?"

"Not sure about that, McCoy. We do know a few deposits were made in Jesus' account. There had to be some way for Hector to collect when the goods were delivered. That was the money he was living on. The money in the account had dwindled almost to zero. He used it to pay Bautch and utilities."

"It is interesting Brent Broderick, my prime suspect, is one of his last customers. It is also interesting the one house on the route I suspected of manufacturing and selling meth is not on the list."

"I have something else for you, McCoy," Dungaree said almost gloating.

"What's that?"

"Well, perhaps you think we are not very thorough investigators. I want you to know we successfully identified footprints in a section of dirt alley, which has some blacktop on it. Not an easy task, mind you! Well, sir, two footprints stood out because of their size. You have interest in both of these men – Axle and Brent. I wondered which of the boots exactly matched the footprints we found closest to the body. We got a print from Axle when he was at our station for questioning. His boot did not match," he said, elated.

"Boy!" McCoy said, and he rubbed his chin. "Anything else?"

"Why yes, Brent's son had a high level of alcohol in him when the crash occurred. We also ran some drug tests – seems the boy had a little coke and heroin in him. We wondered where he got those last substances because pot and meth are easy for kids to get, but not necessarily coke and heroin," Dungaree concluded.

"Yes, and daddy dear was one of Hector's customers for both drugs. Perhaps he thought his boy just got a bad batch, or perhaps he is using Hector for a scapegoat for selling him the stuff," McCoy summarized and then sadly looked out the window.

Dungaree followed his gaze. Both seasoned investigators knew in their guts they had distressingly found the killer of Hector.

Now is the time to prove it without a reasonable doubt.

CHAPTER EIGHTEEN
BRENT
...FREEDOM FROM BONDAGE...

Ellen woke to sunshine streaming through her bedroom's priscilla curtains. "Oh how wonderful, a bright sunshiny day," she exclaimed out loud, waking both Sweetie Pie, who had been sound asleep next to her, and Buttercup on her large cushion on the floor. After stretching and yawning, Ellen and her pets hopped out of bed and headed to the kitchen.

I know it is Wednesday, but I just don't feel like hustling and going to yoga this morn, Ellen thought as she let Buttercup out the back door. She started coffee before letting Buttercup back in. Then she and her pets trotted downstairs to the basement. After feeding them, Ellen went back upstairs, poured a cup of coffee, put cereal, fruit and milk in a bowl and grabbed her notebook to write her daily letter to the "Universe."

In it Ellen noted how much had happened since she wrote her letter before finding Hector's body swinging on her yellow chain. It seemed so obvious to her. In a rage, Axle had killed him. But after talking with BB, she knew in her heart he did not. As she sat there, she began to think oh, my, Annie even told me Brent goes to work shortly after Sam and his wife leave for their paper route. I see now how Brent would have had time to kill Hector and then leave for work. But I got distracted when I overheard Yah-Yah Girl talk about the tree trimmer and drugs. Maybe her brother-in-law, or whatever he is to her, did it. Sure seems to me drugs are being made next door. All I know is I want this to end soon. Our tour day is almost here. I'm scared because I know the killer is loose and lives very close to me. Thank goodness for the sunshine. I'm grateful too, because it doesn't appear the crabapple blossoms are frozen on my tree. She asked the Universe to help her work through the problems today. After completing her letter, Ellen got up, put her dishes in the sink and went back to her bedroom.

She threw on jeans, a sweatshirt, and a jacket. She headed to the back door and yelled at her dog, "Hey, Buttercup, want to go for a walk?" The dog bounded to her side. Snatching Buttercup's leash and a poop bag, the two headed out the door. I'm going to walk the tour route and see how the crabapples are doing, she thought. This is such a typical spring day here: rapidly melting snow and brilliant sunshine. I have a hunch the blossoms are going to be just fine.

As she neared Brent's house, which was close to the end of the route, a woman and two little girls came out of the front door, headed to one of the cars.

A few seconds later, Brent came out on the front porch, angrily yelling at the woman, "Go ahead and leave, bitch. I won't be here when you get back." He threw a large pot at her. It grazed her head and then shattered when it hit the ground.

The little girls were crying and one of the woman's eyes was black. She clutched her head and shaking, hustled the girls into the car and helped them get into their car seats. Dressed in professional clothes, Ellen guessed she was taking the girls to daycare before going to work.

After she drove off, Brent went back into his house. Ellen pulled her phone from her pocket and called McCoy. "Mark, I know we were going to get together around 10:30, but if you can, come sooner. I just witnessed a distressing scene with Brent and his wife. She just left with her kids in the car."

"I'm in a meeting, Ellen, but I will be there very

soon. I'll call the officer, who is close to your house, and ask him to tail Mrs. Broderick. Please describe her car for me."

"It's a gray older Chevy sedan. There are two little girls in car seats in the back."

"Thanks, Ellen. I'll be at your house shortly."

Within the hour, McCoy knocked on Ellen's door.

"Thank you for coming so quickly, Captain McCoy. I know you probably want to talk to me about what happened yesterday and why my cousin and I were in that building."

"You're right, Ellen, I do want to find that out, but first can you tell me what you witnessed this morning?"

Ellen explained what she saw, "You know it is strange I saw Brent because he usually goes to work much earlier."

"Yes, that is interesting, Ellen, and astute on your part. Have you ever attended a citizen police academy or something of that nature?"

"No. But early in my public relations and marketing career, I belonged to the Colorado Public Information Officers' Association because I worked for an emergency services nonprofit. I did get some training through the association because my organization was involved in numerous fires, a couple of tornadoes, major snow storms, and two or three bad plane crashes. In those incidences, I had to report to the command center and coordinate our media responses with the other organizations and the police commander."

"I see. So, you do have some police experience," McCoy stated, picking up his phone ringing in his jacket. "McCoy here. I see. Thank you.

Yes, please continue to follow her and report back to me. Ellen, thank you for letting me know about what you saw this morn. I have to leave now. We can continue this conversation just as soon as I can."

McCoy got up and walked out of Ellen's house. He called Dungaree. "I'm going to interview Broderick now instead of this afternoon. For some reason, he is home. I need for you and Green to provide me backup. I want you stationed in the alley in an unmarked car, and Green in a squad car on the street about a block away. Can you both be there within the half hour?"

"Sure, McCoy. But what about the cop providing surveillance for Ellen?"

"He's tailing Mrs. Broderick. She dropped her kids off at daycare and is now heading to work."

"Okay. Green and I will be there pronto. I'll let you know when we are in place."

A short time later, Dungaree contacted McCoy and let him know he and Green were in position.

McCoy parked his car in front of Brent's house. The lights in the house were on.

He pressed the doorbell, but it did not ring. Probably broken, he thought. I bet there are a lot of busted things in this house. He then loudly knocked on the door. Brent opened it and looked surprised, perhaps expecting to see his wife there ready for another round of fighting or one of Axle's workers at the wrong house.

When Brent saw McCoy, his expression turned to one of suspicion. This man did not look like somebody who would work for Axle. "What do you want," he annoyingly and brusquely barked.

"Police officer Mark McCoy, Mr. Broderick. I would like to have a few words with you."

"A few words about what, McCoy? I'm busy!"

"It's part of our investigation about the murder

162

in the alley, sir," McCoy said softly and calmly. Brent seemed to quiet down some and then replied, "Well, I can talk with you tomorrow."

McCoy knew he was hedging for time and there was a good chance he would skip out on him. "I'm afraid that won't work. May I come in?"

"What do you mean it won't work? And no, you can't come in," he shouted.

"Mmmmm," McCoy almost whispered. "Well, if you prefer, you can come down to my office."

"I'm not going to your office, and I don't have to talk with you," Brent emphatically stated.

McCoy calmly replied, "Well, you don't have to talk with me. You have a right to have an attorney present. As far as going to my office, I do have the authority to take you as a person of interest for questioning. Now, what would you prefer: A visit in your living room or an interrogation at headquarters?"

Brent begrudgingly opened the screen door and motioned McCoy to come in. The room was a mess: toys strewn everywhere, dirty dishes on the side tables and on the floor, pieces of clothing and shoes on the furniture. McCoy noticed a pair of large men's boots in one corner.

McCoy looked at Brent and said, "Where would you like me to sit?"

"Oh, any place you would like, McCoy," Brent sneered. McCoy sat on the couch. Brent sat in a chair opposite him.

McCoy said, "Here is my card," and carefully reached in his pocket to pull out a business card. His phone was in there too, and unobtrusively, he hit a button to alert Dungaree, who was stationed in the alley, that he was in the house. He handed the card to Brent, who looked at it. Then, McCoy sat back and took another good long look at Brent.

He was dressed in blue jeans and a button down shirt which was only buttoned in a few places, showing his hairy chest. Brent's dark hair was disheveled, and he had heavy stubble on his face. He was barefoot. This guy is big, thought McCoy. Maybe not as quite as big as Axle, but close. I'd guess 6 foot 3 or 4 inches, a good 230 pounds and a size 12 shoe. He also looked pretty hung over, with baggy red eyes. He asked, "Your name is?"

"Broderick – Brent. I own this house."

"I see, and you live here with your wife and some kids?"

"Yeah, my wife and two little brats!"

McCoy thought of the two little girls Ellen saw. She said they were precious and scared. He felt really sorry for Brent's family. "And where are they now?"

"Wife took the kids to daycare and then she went to work. She's an administrative assistant for the Lavoy Company."

"I see. Who do you work for, Mr. Broderick?"

"Cut out the "Mr." part, McCoy. I work for Fort Logan Mental Hospital. I'm a guard and also do some maintenance. Work the 6 a.m. to 3 p.m. shift. Not feeling too well today, so I called in sick. That's why I don't have a lot of time, McCoy. I need to get to bed."

"Worked there long, Broderick?"

"Just a couple of years. I retired from the Army several years ago and worked out at Fitzsimons."

"That's a good little distance from here."

"Yeah, my first wife had a job at Swedish Hospital, that's why we moved here. The commute for me got longer and longer with the zillions of people moving in."

"So how long were you married the first time, Broderick?"

"About 8 years. Just long enough so she can get some of my pension."

"You seem pretty resentful about it."

"Yeah, that slut."

"She left you for another man?"

"Well, it wasn't for another woman!" Brent said angrily. "She left and took our son with her. At least I got the house."

"Mmmm, I see." Fort Logan is a lot closer to your home than Fitzsimons."

"Yeah."

"So did you see any active duty when you were in the Army?"

"Yeah-Bosnia – tank patrol. I was just 20. Got blown up. Hurt pretty bad. That is how I met my first wife. They sent me to the VA Hospital here, where she was working." Brent reported.

"I'm sorry."

"It was awful, and I was a long way from home, as if it mattered."

"Where did you grow up?"

"Cincinnati," Brent responded with another sneer.

"Take it your home life in Cincinnati wasn't too great?"

"Yep – I went through several foster homes. My dad is still locked up, and I have no idea where my mom is. She didn't want me, for sure. Her other kids were taken from her. The Army seemed like a great way out."

McCoy thought of Axle next door and how he came to the same conclusion about the military.

"Learn any skills in the Army?"

"Not really, except for sharp shooting and a little mechanical work."

"Sounds like good skills for your current job at Ft. Logan. I know the mental hospital is very old and the grounds are extensive."

"Yeah, I guess so."

"And your son, Todd?" McCoy softly asked.

Brent looked at him with an incredulous stare. "Amazing you brought up my dead son. What does this have to do with the investigation?"

"Sorry to have to bring this up, Brent. My job is to get as much background information as I can. That is why I asked about your wife's job. I'm sure this is painful for you. Can you tell me how and when he died?"

"A car accident, last fall, he was only sixteen," Brent replied and choked up.

"Sorry, man," McCoy stated. "Was he the driver?"

"Yeah," Brent barked out, "Killed all four of them in the car not far from here," Brent wiped his eyes.

"We're about done here, Brent. Can you give me your wife's business number?"

"What do you need it for?" he barked. "A cozy little chit-chat with my wife, just you and her?"

McCoy dodged the insinuation and calmly replied, "We are interviewing all the neighbors. I will have a female police representative with me, Brent."

"Well, I told you where she worked. You can look up the number yourself. She doesn't know nothin'. Just look at the mess of this house. She doesn't do anything and those brats cry all the time."

"Calm down, Brent. I know this has been tough and the murder in the alley did not help, I am sure," McCoy said as he got up to leave.

Brent stood up to and came over to him. "Don't mess with my wife, McCoy!"

McCoy stood his ground and stared him in the eye. Then he calmly walked out the door.

When he got in his car, using his hands-free phone, he called LaVoy and Company and asked for the human resources director. When Sue Smith got on the line, he explained who he was and stated he had reason to believe Brent's wife was in immediate danger. He asked her to bring Joan into her office immediately, and he and another inspector would be there shortly. "Please make sure she does not get or make any calls. Also, alert your security guard. I will supply additional security in the parking lot in case her husband shows up." He hung up the phone.

He saw Brent watching from the window. He did not know if Brent was aware of the phone conversation since he did not have a phone to his ear. He slowly drove off and parked down the street. He then contacted Dungaree in the alley, and told him to keep surveillance on Brent and he'd contact Green to stay at the main entrance gate of LaVoy and Company.

In the alley, Dungaree started his unmarked car shortly after noticing the sliding doors of Brent's oversized red garage were releasing. Before they were fully opened, Brent started driving his large pick-up truck out of the enclosure. Dungaree noticed his neighbor, Sam, was in his driveway with one of his dogs on a leash.

Suddenly, Ellen appeared in her driveway and started walking towards Sam. Brent saw her, gunned the pick-up, drove up to her, rolled down his window and yelled, "Get in here. You are exactly who I need as a hostage."

Dungaree veered his car in between Brent's truck and Ellen and yelled, "Ellen, the back door is unlocked, get in the car and fall to the floor. I don't know if this guy is armed or not."

Brent swerved around Dungaree's car and swiftly accelerated his truck up the little alley, which intersected the alley off Ellen's driveway.

Sam ran back to his home, called 911 and tried to convey as best he could with his voice box what had just happened.

Dungaree called McCoy and explained what Brent did. McCoy responded, "Tell Ellen she has a choice: She can get out after you pull over, or she can accompany you as a police citizen assistant. I learned this morn she used to belong to the PIO Association. Then get to LaVoy pronto, using your lights and siren. I am tailing Broderick now. Green will meet you at LaVoy. I have already talked with their HR department."

From the back seat, Ellen yelled, "I'm with you, Dungaree."

"Okay, Ellen. You can get up now, put your seat belt on and keep a look out for Broderick. I don't want him to see us with these lights and sirens I am using to get through stop lights and signs. He may get spooked and drive erratic."

Next, McCoy called Sue Smith back and asked her to get the name and phone number of the daycare where Brent's kids were. Joan was in her office and was able to immediately relay the info to him. McCoy called the daycare director and informed her Brent's children were in immediate danger of their father. She was not to release them to him under any circumstances. He was sending an officer to the facility in case Brent showed up.

He called another officer and told him to get to the Humpty Dumpty Preschool and Daycare.

A call came in from 911 dispatcher about a message from a citizen concerned about an incident in the alley. "Let him know his neighbor is okay," McCoy instructed.

Nearing the entrance to LaVoy and Company, he called Dungaree. "Where are you? I see. Meet me two blocks over and ask Ellen to get into my car. Then wait just outside of LaVoy's gate in a location where Brent can't see you."

The two cars rendezvoused, Ellen jumped out of Dungaree's car and into McCoy's. "Why do you want me to accompany you, McCoy?"

"With any luck, I will be talking with Joan shortly. I will tell her I can have a female police officer come into the interview with me or you, who happens to be a police citizen assistant. I will explain time is of the essence and it will take some time to get Officer Catherine Govy, a domestic violence expert here. She will be assisting Joan once a domestic violence complaint is signed. Are you okay with this, Ellen?"

"Yes. I have helped other women sign just such a complaint because they called me for support."

The security guard met McCoy and Ellen at the entrance. "A distraught husband, who I suspect is armed and dangerous, will be arriving shortly. Our officers are tailing him now and will be arriving shortly. They will station in the parking lot. I will be in contact with you and the officers once Ms. Lane and I and are inside the building. In the meantime, an alert is being sent by HR to all employees of "a possible dangerous situation," instructing them to remain in the building. No vendors or others should be allowed past the gate."

McCoy quickly drove to the main entrance, and they got out. A woman in a dark business suit came up to them and introduced herself as Sue Smith. "Officer McCoy, let's step into this side office so you can fill me in on what's happening," she said. He and Ellen followed Smith.

"We have a domestic violence situation on our hands. I am hoping Joan will press charges, and we can get her and her children to a safe house. Her husband is also 'a person of interest' in a murder which happened in Ellen's alley a couple of days ago," McCoy explained. "Ellen is a neighbor and is a trained citizen police assistant. We will wait for a domestic violence police officer to arrive if that is what Joan prefers. I'm afraid we don't have much time, ladies. Just got a text from the surveillance officers that Brent is almost here. We need to talk to Joan right away and get her to safety."

Sue Smith ushered them to her neat office and led them to an inner office where two women sat. She said, "Thank you, Amanda," and her assistant left.

McCoy looked at Joan. She was crying softly. Her hair was a mess, and he could see bruise marks on her face. "Joan, for now, your kids are safe, and so are you. I'm Officer Mark McCoy, and I believe you have seen your neighbor who is a citizen police assistant and helping me until a domestic violence officer arrives."

Ellen went up to her. Joan stood up and rushed to the older woman. "Oh, Ellen, I am so sorry Brent would not let me meet with you about the fudge sale."

"Oh honey, don't worry about that. I am so glad you are here. I have been so concerned ever since the night I heard your scream." She and Joan hugged each other.

"You heard me scream, Ellen?"

"Don't be embarrassed, Joan. I knew what that scream was about because I have screamed like that myself. It took me a while to realize it was you."

Joan turned her attention to McCoy. "Why are you here? What did Brent do?"

He explained Ellen had been walking her dog by Joan's house earlier in the day. She saw how Brent behaved as Joan was trying to leave with her daughters. "Ellen called me as soon as she could. I was going to interview him today about the murder in the alley but decided to do it sooner."

Joan whimpered. "Oh, no."

McCoy replied, "We can talk about that later, Joan, for now we need to get you and the children in a permanent safe situation. We have officers at their school and the director knows what is happening. We are tailing Brent. He is driving his truck here now, as we speak. We have backups in the parking lot. Joan, in order for us to help you and your kids, we need for you to press domestic charges by signing this statement."

Joan began to cry. Ellen moved closer to her and put her arm around her. "It's going to be okay, Joan, trust me. Lots of women have gone through this and now have good lives. You will, too."

McCoy's phone beeped. He answered and told the ladies, "Brent is in the parking lot. Joan will you help us, yourself and your children?"

Somewhere deep inside of her, courage came and she resolutely said, "Yes." Ellen gave her the document, which Sue Smith had printed off her computer. Joan boldly signed.

McCoy's phone beeped again. He dashed out of Smith's office and ran to the front door. The guard was there. His face looked as white as the snow capped Rockies. "Stand back," McCoy said. He opened the door and met a surprised and startled Brent. Two officers immediately rushed up to him from behind. "Brent Broderick, I am arresting you on a charge of domestic violence, driving under the influence and suspicion of the murder of Hector Hernandez," Brent reached for his pocket, but an officer grabbed him. McCoy noticed he was wearing his boots.

171

CHAPTER NINETEEN
THE WIVES AND THE ALLIGATOR
... *IT IS HARD TO HAVE THE FORTITUDE TO LEAVE. ABUSERS PRESSURE THEIR VICTIMS OR PERSUADE THEM TO RETURN WITH PROMISES THEY NEVER KEEP...*

Back in Sue Smith's office, McCoy informed the group Brent had been arrested. "Thank you, Joan. Our domestic violence officer is on her way. Ellen and I will leave now, but I will be in touch later today."

Joan squeezed Ellen's hand. "You have been so helpful to me. I never would have dreamed you had been a victim of domestic abuse. Ellen, you are so smart and so beautiful. I hope I can be like you when I am a lady-of-a-certain age. I wish you could stay with me."

"Joan, I will keep in touch with you. And I don't know about being smart and beautiful, but I do know your life will improve dramatically now you have taken this step and after you get help and support. You will need it because it is hard to have the fortitude to leave. Abusers are known to pressure their victims or persuade them to return with ridiculous promises they never keep."

When she and McCoy got back to his car, he asked, "Ellen, it is important to talk with Brent's first wife. I will try and set up an appointment now. Will you come with me?"

"Oh, why not, McCoy? That interview can't be any harder than this one. While you're contacting her, I would like to call my cousin and let her know I am okay and will fill her in."

"Go ahead, Ellen."

McCoy did not relish talking to Brent's first wife, Lavonne Broderick. She had recently lost a teenage son, age 16. Boys of this age could be cruel to their mothers, he knew. Her former husband, Brent, was now headed to jail on a domestic violence charge and suspicion of murder. He contacted Tom Hughes, the human resources vice president at Swedish Hospital.

"Yes, Lavonne is our head nurse of surgery, and she is in today. Certainly, I will ask her to come to my office and brief her about your request to talk with her. Of course, she will not be docked for time for the police interview. Fortunately, no major surgeries are planned until later today."

Lavonne had a good job, an important job, a job that paid well. An attractive woman, with dark hair, Lavonne came into Hughes' office and shook McCoy's hand. He introduced her to Ellen, explaining her role as a citizen police assistant.

"Yes, Ellen, Nancy has told me all about your Pink Blossoms Garden and Neighborhood Tour in honor of Mamie. Nancy has been a big support to me. I didn't know you were a citizen police assistant. How exciting that must be."

"I'm going to leave you alone," Hughes said. "Take as long as you would like. No one can hear your conversation here. Lavonne, if you choose to go home after this, I'll arrange for you to go with no time docked." He walked out of the office and closed the door.

Lavonne fixed her gaze on McCoy and waited for him to speak. "Ms. Broderick, I am sorry to have to bring you into this investigation, and I know of your recent loss of your son, Todd." Lavonne's face darkened. "I know this has to be painful, but I would like to know a little bit about Todd and your relationship to him this past year."

"What does my son have to do with the murder in the alley, me or even Brent?" she demanded, a woman used to barking questions and getting answers.

"Well for one thing, we know the man who was murdered sold drugs to your ex-husband, and we know at the time of his death your son had more than alcohol in his system. He had Class IV drugs, specifically coke and heroin. We have records of Brent buying these types of drugs from the victim, and we find it interesting a 16-year-old boy's autopsy noted them."

Lavonne let out a soft wail. "So that's where Todd got the drugs?"

"We don't know for sure. That is why I am here today to talk with you. Please tell us about your relationship with your son the past year or so."

Lavonne's whole appearance changed. Gone was the look of a confident woman, used to being in charge. Before McCoy and Ellen now was a sad woman whose gaze was at the floor, she was wringing her hands, and seemed to be making an enormous effort not to cry. When she raised her head, there were tears floating in her big green eyes, close to the banks of her eye lids, about to escape their banks.

"It was awful. He was belligerent. I had no control over him. His grades dropped dramatically. He drank all the time. I suspected he was an alcoholic like his father. He spent more and more time with him even though this was against the court order. Brent gave him a car. He said Todd needed it because of the long hours I worked. I didn't see my son much his last year, and when I did, he was confrontational and rude. He never hit me, like his father did many times when I was married to him, but I feared he would. He was about Brent's size when he died. I had so many hopes and dreams for him. I extricated myself from that abusive marriage and made a good life for me and Todd. I thought he would go into the medical profession like me. I don't know what happened. I just could not control Todd anymore." Lavonne started sobbing.

"There, there," McCoy said in a soothing voice. Ellen reached out her hand to her, and Lavonne grabbed it. "You are correct. You did not cause your son's addiction, you could not cure it, and you could not control it, even if you were bigger than Todd. You did all you could to give him and you a good life. I'm so sorry, Lavonne. You are a brave woman, and I so appreciate the time you took to talk with me. I know it took a lot of courage to tell me about your son and his behavior."

They sat still for awhile. Lavonne was regaining her composure and McCoy was deeply touched by this mother and all the mothers he had known who had lost sons to substances they had no control over.

"Anything else, Officer?" Lavonne said.

"No, you answered all my questions, Lavonne."

"Good," she said and sat up straight and the appearance of an efficient nurse returned. "Then I'll go back to the floor, Officer. At least there I can help cure and control. We certainly do our best not to cause – do no harm, you know."

They got up and walked out the door.

As Ellen and McCoy walked to his car, he called Officer Catherine Govey, the domestic violence officer who was helping Joan. "Just got done talking with Broderick's first wife, Lavonne, about her son."

"That must not have been a walk in the park, Mark."

"It wasn't. I think part of her story is Todd died of alcohol. She sure knew about the drugs, but letting people know about them would have been further shame for her. I imagine she has kept herself together while Todd was growing up by hard work and trying to do the best for him, hoping all along his father's addictive genes were not present. I need to talk further with Joan Broderick. Can you tell me where she is now?"

"She and her kids are scheduled to be in a shelter for twenty-one days. We will soon be headed to her house. She is getting clothes for her and the kids. I can let Sue Smith know you want to talk further with her. We can wait for you here. If you can, bring Ellen that would be great. Joan really bonded with her."

"Okay. Are the kids still at – what was it, Humpty Dumpty?"

"Yes. With their dad in jail today, I felt the kids were safe there and would be one part of their lives that would be stable. It is a good school, Mark. Joan has a good head on her shoulders when it is not being rattled by her husband."

McCoy and Ellen drove back to LaVoy and went into Sue Smith's office.

Joan looked up and ran to give Ellen a hug. "Oh, Ellen, I am glad you are back. I understand the police officer wants to talk with me further."

"Captain McCoy does. If it will help, you can hold my hand."

"Thank you, Ellen."

"I am afraid I must ask you a few more questions," McCoy said softly looking at her. She seemed somewhat rested, her hair was combed, and she looked a little more at ease.

"Alright, Officer. First, I can't tell you how much I am grateful for everything you, Catherine and Ellen have done for me and my girls." She paused, and looked at Ellen. "Thank you for coming back to be with me Ellen. I know this is above and beyond your citizen duties. I don't know what would have happened to us if I continued to live with Brent." She started to cry.

"I'm so glad you are in a safe place, Joan," McCoy said. "I want you to know I talked with Lavonne. Seems Brent had a pattern for how he treated his wives."

Joan nodded. "We never talked. She came to the house a couple of times, looking for Todd or telling him he had to come home. I stayed out of her way."

"Yes, she told me in the past year or so Todd had changed, and even though there was a court order about parental time, Todd, himself, did not abide by that. What can you tell me about Todd, Joan?"

"He was a very angry kid. I did not confront nor discipline him. I would not let the girls near him. After his dad bought a car for him from Axle next door, Todd was at the house almost every day. He and his father spent a lot of time in the garage. Seems like the only time Brent was happy was when Todd was here. Brent does not have any friends. Todd was his friend."

"Do you know what they did in the garage, Joan?"

"Besides talking, they smoked a lot and drank. I know Brent should not have done that with his son. I was petrified of Brent and Todd, too, for that matter," she said.

McCoy told her, "The dead man, Hector Hernandez, was a drug dealer and had worked for a large drug ring before we captured all the members except for Hector." Joan's eyes opened wide. "We found a list of his customers. Your husband's name is on the list. What can you tell me about Brent and drugs, Joan?"

"He has PTSD, you know. I bet most Bosnian

vets do. The things they saw in that war were awful! I never knew what would set him off. Sometimes a loud noise would really upset him. I know Brent smoked pot and snorted a little meth to help with the anxiety. It was always scary when he got his gun out. Sometimes he would go to the back of our yard and just point the gun at a tree. I don't know why. He hated squirrels. But his gun is meant for killing something much larger than a little squirrel," she said, starting to cry harder.

McCoy remembered Ellen telling him about a man in the alley pointing a gun at a tree one Thanksgiving morning. "I see. That must have been harrowing for you. I don't know if you know this, but Todd's autopsy showed he had more than alcohol in his blood when he died."

Joan starred at him. "Did he have meth, too?" she gasped.

"There were traces of meth, but the coke and heroin were of most interest to me. While working for this police department, I have never had the instance of a kid with those drugs in his system."

Joan gasped again. "Where did he get them?" she demanded.

"We suspect from Brent since Hector's records show he sold your husband more than pot and meth."

Joan began to wail. "That poor kid. He just wanted to have a father, and his father just wanted to have a friend."

Both Ellen and Catherine went to her and held her. When she quieted down some, McCoy said, "I'll be in touch, Joan. Catherine, with Ellen's help, I bet, will guide you on the path to a much better life."

He and Ellen quietly left the room. After thanking Sue Smith, they headed to McCoy's car.

They no sooner got in the car when McCoy's phone started to beep. The caller ID indicated who it was.

"Yeah, Dungaree, what's up?"

"You know, McCoy, I'm guessing Ft. Logan owns alligator loppers. They have many trees on the property. Hell, Brent might have even had the purchasing agent buy them for him. I bet he is quite skilled at operating one."

"Good point, Dungaree. Hadn't thought of that. I was under the impression Axle taught him when they cut down the tree in his yard. Bet Brent is 'quite adept' in wielding an alligator lopper, too."

While McCoy was on the phone, Ellen called her cousin. "Yes, I'm okay, but exhausted. Oh, thank you for offering to bring dinner by. We can eat on my patio. I have lots to catch you up on, and I know we have a final strategy meeting with the tour planning committee in the morning. We need to make sure all loose ends are taken care of and answer any concerns they have about the murderer. Thank you, Murph. Yes, red wine. You know, 'Red, red wine makes me feel so fine.'" She hung up and then sheepishly looked at McCoy.

"You have been so helpful today, Ellen. I could see you really connected with Joan and Lavonne," McCoy said as he pulled up to Ellen's pretty yellow house with black shutters. Murph's sexy red car was parked in front. "I know you and Murph will have a great dinner and visit. Please have an extra glass of red wine for me. I'll contact you tomorrow and let you know what's happening."

"Thanks, Mark," Ellen said. She slowly got out of the door and realized how tired she was. She could hardly wait to open her front door and see her cousin, Buttercup and Sweetie Pie.

McCoy headed to Smith and turned at the corky

alley on Olive. He was in luck. Axle was in his garage tinkering with one of his cars. McCoy pulled into his driveway, stopped the car and got out. "Hello, Axle," he said.

Axle looked up in disbelief. "Now what, McCoy?"

"Easy, Axle. Just want a little info on alligator loppers."

"What?" Axle almost screamed.

"I just want to know how to start one and how noisy it is. Personally, I have never had the pleasure of operating one. Frankly, the trees in my yard are a mess. They could use a little attention from me."

"I'm not buying this bullshit, McCoy. But to get you out of here – like pronto – I'll show you. I had to buy another, you know, since you took mine. By the way, I don't want it back, but some compensation, I think, is justified," Axle said.

"I'll make sure you get it back." Axle walked over to his shelf. McCoy marveled at the neatness of his garage and the muscular structure of this man. Hell, he could be a model in GQ, he thought. Not one of Axle's muscles rippled when he picked up the tool. Axle brought it out to the drive way and grabbed a thick branch from the trailer attached to his truck.

"We use this when an electric one won't work on a job. It's just not as powerful, nor efficient. Any girl could operate this, McCoy." He pressed the start button, pried open the handles which were in each hand, slid the blades, jaws, on the branch and then brought his hands together. Thump. The branch was cut in two. "Because this guy cuts from side-to-side, not up and down like a chain saw, it is possible to cut just a little way in and stop if you want or if you want to just get a start on a really strong piece of wood, say an oak or hawthorn branch."

"Also," McCoy added, "The saw would not have to be on very long. It is pretty quiet, but would be louder if you kept it on for a number of minutes."

"That's right, McCoy. Maybe that is why his head was not completely severed or maybe the killer heard something, turned off the alligator, and ran," Axle stated with a satisfied look on his face.

"Thanks, Axle. Most helpful," McCoy said, getting in his car and turning his car up the alley toward Olive Street and home.

CHAPTER TWENTY
REVENGE
... HE JUST WANTED TO HAVE A FATHER, AND HIS FATHER JUST WANTED TO HAVE A FRIEND ...

McCoy had his work cut out for him. He needed the killer of Hector Hernandez to confess.

He called Green and Dungaree and asked them to be available the next day for a meeting in his office, and possibly to be part of the interrogation of Brent.

The three gathered in McCoy's office. He had a fresh pot of coffee made and a box of chocolate-iced, raspberry-filled bismarcks ready for them.

"Seems like father and son were talking about other things besides sports in their garage," McCoy said. "I think Daddy was showing sonny-boy how to use crack and heroin. You know, just good bonding with his son. He gave him the gift that keeps on giving – addiction. He supplied him with beer, cigarettes, pot, meth, crack and finally, heroin."

"Yeah, that is obvious, McCoy," Dungaree growled. "So, why did he kill Hector, his supplier?"

"And in such a brutal manner," piped in Green.

"Well, for one, his supply was shut off. Hernandez was getting out of the business, so to speak. The second reason – this is really hard, guys – he needed a scapegoat for his son's death. The drug dealer, who sold him all those products, was just perfect for the role. After all, it was Hector's fault Todd had those drugs in his system. Who knows, Brent may have believed they were bad drugs though he used them, too. Having a nice, big, ragged scapegoat protected him from facing up to his own behavior: supplying drugs to his son, which when mixed with the alcohol he gave him, killed Todd. The boy had no sense of reality when he got behind the wheel of his car with his three friends inside. I think that is why Brent so brutally 'presented the body,' if you will. Ellen's yellow chain provided the perfect prop. I'm guessing when Hector entered Brent's garage, Brent overpowered him. He is so much bigger than Hector. He grabbed him, knocked the air out of him by squeezing him hard, and then delivered a blow to his head. Then Brent swiftly threw him in the front seat and quickly drove the short distance to Ellen's driveway so there would not be a trail of blood from his garage. He knew head wounds start to bleed quickly and profusely. Probably the loppers were in the front seat. We know Hector was already dead when Brent draped the body over the chain and clamped the jaws of the alligator down on his neck and disemboweled, the politically correct word, or 'ripped him a new one, an asshole' with the tree lopper. Just killing Hector wasn't enough because that would not assuage his guilt. He needed to wickedly demonstrate his anger towards Hector."

"Wow," Green said and lowered his head not wanting to show the emotion surging through his body.

Dungaree whistled softly, "I think you nailed it, McCoy."

"It makes sense to me. That is why I need your help. Green, I need you in the room to take over the conversation if I get too worked up. Dungaree, I need you to calmly present the facts of your investigation to Brent and to give me some moral support by your presence," McCoy said.

"Alrighty," spoke up Dungaree. "You are an expert, McCoy."

183

"Something I think will help us is Brent hasn't had any alcohol or drugs for at least 24 hours. I don't think he is feeling too well, and this should take some of the fight out of him, hopefully. The prison medics are watching him carefully. He is well enough for the interview. Our appointment with him is at 3:30 p.m. today, guys."

Leaning back in his chair, McCoy went on, "Dungaree, I've contacted Fort Logan Mental Health Hospital. They will release all of their alligator and tree loppers to you." He reached for a drawer in his desk and pulled a large plastic bag out with a pair of big boots in it. "Here are Brent's boots. Can you confirm they match the foot prints you found in the alley?"

"Boots are no problem, but I don't know if we will still discover prints on the loppers. We'll see what we can find. I'll ask everyone in the lab to put their work on hold so we can get to the loppers right away. Late yesterday we started to scour Brent's truck in search of any blood."

"Thanks, Dungaree."

"Green, I'll call Fort Logan's Human Resources director again and get a copy of his application file. I wonder if they did drug testing when he was hired, and I wonder if they did any ongoing testing. Can you visit with the director about any knowledge of Brent's PTSD? I don't think they will give us his medical records at this time. Seems strange to me that they would not be monitoring him since he is a Bosnian vet. It's sad he worked for an organization that helps so many others with PTSD. I did not know that Joan knew about his condition. Maybe she just speculated since he acted like he had it."

"Sure, McCoy. If we could get a copy of his service records, it would be very helpful. Wonder if there is anyone in the area who served with him?"

"Excellent ideas, Green. See what you can gather up."

Later that day, the three men entered the interrogation room, which was painted a cold white with brushed steel furniture and surrounded with two-way mirrors. Cameras were placed at all four corners and strategically placed microphones picked up every sound. Bottles of water were placed on the table near each of the four chairs. There were no windows in the room.

Promptly at 3:30 p.m., two prison guards escorted Brent into the room. He was wearing an orange prison suit. His skin had a yellow hue and his gait was laborious. McCoy met him and said, "Hi, Brent. Please have a seat here," he pointed to a chair at the head of the table. "Let me introduce Inspector Green, who works in my office and Officer Michael Drysten, who heads up our forensic division. He and his staff are recognized throughout the state for their thoroughness. Both of these men have been helping mc with the Hector Hernandez case." With the mention of Hector's name, Brent scowled.

"So to get started here, I have asked Inspector Green to read you your rights."

Green read the standard statement, and Brent replied, "No, goddamn it, I don't want any lawyers here."

"Okay," said McCoy, evenly. "By law, I am to inform you this interrogation session is being recorded and video taped for your protection and ours. Anything you say can be used against you in a court of law."

"Let's get on with this," Brent stated. "I want to get out of here and back to work and go home and visit with my wife. You bastards know I did not kill that Spic. I don't even know why he was in the alley. Axle hires them because they are cheap labor. What about Axle? Why isn't he in jail? He had the equipment to kill that guy."

McCoy replied, "Well, that is what we initially thought too, Brent. As you know, we did question Axle. We let him go as our investigation proceeded."

Again, the cops observed Brent did not look well. He looked like someone towards the end of a vicious hangover. His face was a pasty color of yellow cream, and despite all of his brusqueness, he did not seem to have much energy.

McCoy stated, "I'll just summarize briefly what we know about the victim's background. Hector Hernandez was born in this country and for a long time worked at a restaurant where his mother was employed. He had gone to a community college and studied bookkeeping. After his mother's death, Hernandez quit the restaurant. Brent, do you remember the drug bust in your alley?"

"I sure do. Those bastards in our nice little neighborhood."

"Well, I was the officer in charge and was delighted when we put Jesus Manzanerez behind bars for many years. Funny though, we never found his operation. We got a tip Manzanerez may have had an office and warehouse not far from the sports stadium in one of those old buildings by the tracks. Officer, why don't you tell Brent about that?"

Drysten cleared his throat. "With the help of various utility companies, we were able to identify several possible buildings that still had active tenets because bills were being paid for electricity, gas, water and sewer. Our officers, on a cold and snowy day, were checking these places out. In one of them, a man was obviously in distress. The officers went in and rescued the man from certain death. They called the detox unit who transferred the man to general hospital. These policemen took a look around and found computers, lists and shelves where product had been stored. They brought those items into headquarters. The information reveled this had been Jesus' old operation, and Hector had been serving as the bookkeeper and inventory control manager. We got complete lists of all the customers and found out the inventory, primarily marijuana, meth, coke and heroin, had all been depleted."

Brent's eyes opened wide and he appeared to be about ready to vomit.

"Another piece of the investigation included footprint and autopsy analysis," Drysten went on. "We established a match for the large footprints we found in the alley. Not an easy task, mind you, because some of the alley is paved and some of it is dirt. Also, there is a lot of foot traffic due to Axle's business. Mr. Hernandez' autopsy was most revealing."

"That bastard Hernandez was using drugs, too!" Brent interrupted.

"No," the officer calmly stated. "There were no drugs in his body, and his organs only indicated a mild use of alcohol. What was of interest to us is Hector Hernandez did not die of the obvious injuries to his neck and bowel. He was dead before his body had been mutilated. Because we did not find any trace of blood in the alley until we got to Ms. Lane's driveway, it appears he was killed close to where he was found and then draped over the chain. The killer made an extraordinary effort to mutilate the body."

Brent looked more ill than when he came into the room. His eyes darted from one man to another, his feet tapped, and he was quivering.

McCoy stood up. "So we knew because of the

187

brutal presentation of the body, and the obvious implication that Axle or one of his workers killed Hernandez, that we were dealing with a crime of passion, Brent. Someone who was extremely distraught."

Green thought it would be best to step in and relieve Brent's focus on McCoy. "In our office we carefully reviewed those lists we found in the old building, talked to as many people as we could and looked at another autopsy report."

McCoy, garnering some internal strength said, "That's right, Brent. We found your name on those lists. Seems like you were one of Hector's last customers. You bought pot, meth, coke, heroin and cocaine."

Brent started to get up but a guard put his hand on his shoulder.

Drysten spoke up, "Of course, we thoroughly scrubbed for prints on the loppers Axle turned over to us. We did not find any. The boots you had on yesterday matched perfectly the footprints in the alley." He held up the bag containing the large work boots.

After several minutes of silence, McCoy started talking, "A real surprise to me was another autopsy report besides Hernandez' that we looked at. The autopsy report of your son."

McCoy paused, watching Brent carefully as he prepared to go on. "No, it wasn't just alcohol in his blood when he died, but also pot, meth, coke and heroin. Boys in your neighborhood don't have easy access to coke and heroin."

He could see his words were having a big impact on Brent and was afraid the man's survival mode would kick in. McCoy decided to continue. "I talked with Lavonne."

Brent growled, "That bitch!"

"Hang on, Brent," McCoy commanded. "Seems like the visitation rights had been completely ignored, and Todd continually did not obey her. We confirmed with Joan that Todd was spending more and more time at your house, often in the garage with you, Brent."

"Fricking woman," Brent exclaimed.

McCoy lowered his eyes and then using some of Joan's words, softly said, "Seems like Todd wanted to be with a father he had not spent much time with, and you just wanted your son to adore you."

Brent looked up. His eyes were bright red and he was shaking.

Drysten quietly said, "This morning I went to Fort Logan Mental Health Hospital to get all of their loppers to analyze for prints and blood. We found your prints and Hernandez' blood on the alligator loppers. A short time ago, I got word several drops of Hernandez' blood were found near your truck's front door. Not surprising, since blows to the head often result in immediate and excessive bleeding."

The room was quiet. Brent hung his head and put his hands over his eyes.

McCoy stood up and came forward, "We have enough evidence to charge you with murder, and it is likely you would be placed on death row, Brent. The judge would probably go a little easier on you, though, if you confessed to this murder."

Brent began to cry. The fight was out of him. "Yes, that bastard killed my son. I had to kill him," Brent stated through sobs.

Two guards came up behind Brent, helped him out of his chair, and escorted him through the door and back to a jail cell.

Speaking softly, Green let out, "Wow. You were right, McCoy. Brent needed a large, shaggy scapegoat.

Strange as it may sound, I feel sorry for Hector. After all, he had a difficult life and was trying to get on the right path."

Dungaree got up. Reverently hung his head and quietly said, "May he rest in peace."

"Let's gather tomorrow morn to debrief. For now, I want to get with our public information officer and work on a news release. I hope we can get it to the media by the nightly news," McCoy stated. "I imagine yesterday's release about holding a 'person of interest' reduced the anxiety of many people in Englewood. Now, hopefully, they can get a good night's sleep knowing Brent has been charged. I'll give Ellen a call and see if I can stop by on my way home."

About an hour and a half later, McCoy called Ellen.

When she saw his name on her phone, she quickly answered, "Hi, Captain McCoy."

"Are you going to be home in the next little while?"

"Sure. Are you kidding? The tour starts in less than 48 hours. We're in good shape, but there are always so many last minute details, you know."

Shortly after, McCoy drove up to Ellen's cheery yellow house with the black shutters. He noticed her neighbor Kelly's yard looked as unkempt as ever, with blooming bind weed and yellow dandelions everywhere. He noted Annie's yard looked pretty good, but she had missed knocking off with her cane several dandelion heads. He thought to himself, next week I am going to focus on both of these neighbors. I'll see if I can get Annie some help with Englewood's Senior Services program. I will have Dungaree start looking into Kelly's background and get some surveillance detail on the house.

McCoy walked up Ellen's sidewalk and was glad

to see her crabapple tree was budding out beautifully.

She met him at the door. "Captain McCoy. Come on in. Good to see you in my nice warm living room." McCoy chuckled. "That's right. I remember recently seeing you when it was freezing, and I don't think the room in the old warehouse district had been cleaned in a long, long time."

"So, you're on your way home? "

"Yes."

"Does that mean you're off duty?"

"It certainly does, Ellen."

"Well, in that case may I offer you a glass of red wine?

"You may, and that sounds wonderful. Thank you."

"Why don't you have a seat on my couch? You can see the mountains from there. I'll be right back with our beverages."

Ellen returned with two glasses of wine, a small dish of olives and cheese and plates and napkins. "So, I'm wondering what brought you to my humble abode."

McCoy grabbed the wine and took a long slow drink before saying, "I do have news for you, Ellen. I wanted you to hear it before it was broadcast on the nightly news."

"Oh?"

"A little while ago, Brent confessed to the murder of Hector Hernandez."

"Oh, my." Ellen's hand jerked and she almost spilt wine on her green couch.

"We got Fort Logan's supply of various types of loppers. Dungaree found Hector's blood on an alligator one. He also found blood in Brent's truck. It wasn't uncommon for Brent to have the hospital's equipment in his truck. That's why we never found the tree equipment that severed his neck."

Ellen's hazel eyes widened and she softly said, "But why did he kill him and why did he have to leave Hector on my chain?"

"Brent needed a scapegoat for the death of his son since he did not want to acknowledge he supplied the drugs and alcohol that killed him. Alcoholics and drug addicts do not take responsibility for their actions unless they get in recovery. He knew Hector was 'going out of business, so to speak' and could tell someone Brent was his customer. This would cover up the real motive for his decision to kill Hector. The drugs and alcohol Brent supplied his son, along with the car he bought him, guaranteed his son's friendship. Killers sometimes display their victims in crimes of passion. Your chain definitely would bring attention to the crime and the deceased."

"Oh, how awful. Did you contact Lavonne and Joan?"

"Yes. Green visited with each of them personally. As bad as Brent was, he was at one time loved by both of these women and fathered their children."

"What hard emotional work." Ellen slowly finished her wine and looked at the majestic mountain view from her window. "I heard it said one time words don't go into your heart. They sit on top of your heart until it breaks, and then they tumble in."

McCoy nodded and did not say anything for several minutes. "You know, Ellen, I am going to station an officer at each of the alley's entrances on Saturday. Only local traffic will be allowed in. People are so curious. You and your neighbors have had much trauma. You don't need a bunch of people gawking in the alley."

"Thank you, Mark. I need to get word out to the committee and a statement on our web site."

McCoy handed her a copy of the police department's news release. "This information may be helpful. You certainly can link to our site."

"I appreciate both, Captain."

"Thank you, Ellen. By the way, Lynn and I are planning on attending the tour."

"Oh, that is wonderful. Please stay after the tour is officially finished. We are having a celebration in my yard and would love for you and your wife to attend. Also, please invite Officer Green and Dungaree."

"I think both of them are planning on coming. You know, Dungaree is quite a gardener and is very knowledgeable about architecture."

"He's an amazing man," Ellen said and her cheeks turned a little red.

CHAPTER 21
THE PINK BLOSSOMS GARDEN AND NEIGHBORHOOD TOUR
... *A MERRY HEART DOETH GOOD LIKE A MEDICINE, BUT A BROKEN SPIRIT DRIETH THE BONES...*

"Get up. Get up, you sleepy head. Get up. Get up, you sleepy head," Ellen's phone alarm began singing at 5 a.m. sharp. She, Buttercup, and Sweetie Pie all sat up immediately. Ellen grabbed her phone and turned off the alarm. *Don't want to wake Murph up, and who came up with that bright idea for an alarm sound,* she scolded herself. Murph was spending the night at Ellen's because the tour group needed to get everything ready by the time The Pink Blossoms Garden and Neighborhood Tour

started at 9 a.m. The day had finally arrived.

Her cousin, sleeping in the guest room across the hall, fortunately did not hear Ellen and her pets get out of bed and head to the kitchen. "Wow," Ellen exclaimed looking out her kitchen window. *What a sight.* Sunlight was streaming in the window and served as a backlight for the brilliant pink crabapple blossoms on the tree in front of it. Quickly opening the window, the scent of the fragrant blossoms filled the air. "Oh my," Ellen uttered to herself, "What a gorgeous day for our tour. I remember just a couple of days ago thinking the blossoms may have frozen. The snow and cold are now just a vague memory."

Abruptly, Ellen remembered where she and Murphy went that blustery, winter-like day and all of the events leading up to the arrest of Brent Broderick for the murder of Hector Hernandez.

Buttercup nudged her leg hard. The push brought Ellen back to the present moment and the need to let Buttercup out. While her dog was outside, Ellen turned on her oven and checked if the chocolate croissants she had put in there the night before had risen. Oh, what beautiful pastry and from a box, to boot. I'm so glad I thought about surprising Murph with something really special for breakfast today.

After letting the dog in, Ellen went down to her basement and fed both of her animals. When she came back upstairs, she started the coffee. The smell of the baking croissants was wafting through the air. When the coffee was done, she poured a cup and took it with her as she went to the guest bedroom. After knocking on the door and hearing a groan, she opened it and started singing in a loud squeaky voice, "Get up. Get up, you sleepy head. Get up. Get up, you sleepy head."

Murph sat up and smiled at her cousin and after taking the coffee, said, "You're wonderful. Thank you."

In the kitchen nook, the cousins sat down to breakfast at Ellen's round white Formica table. "What a gorgeous site your crabapple blossoms are, Ellen, and what a gorgeous Colorado sunshiny morning," Murph exclaimed.

Their eyes went to the small television Ellen had on her nearby kitchen counter. "Englewood police arrest killer of gruesome murder in a residential alley a couple of weeks ago," the male newscaster stated.

"And just in time," his female co-host added. "Hundreds of people are planning on touring the quaint mid-century-modern neighborhood where the murder took place. Tour guides will explain the distinctive architecture and the unique crabapple trees planted in honor of then First Lady Mamie Eisenhower who grew up in our area."

195

Both Murph's and Ellen's phones began to ring. "Ellen, Nancy here. Our web site sales are going crazy. Do you think we should cap them?"

Murph's real estate company office manager was on her phone with the same question.

Ellen's and Murph's eyes met and both said to the respective callers, "Remember we laughed when we set the limit at 1,000? We're almost there. Let callers know we reached our limit. Get their contact info and let them know next year we will contact them first for our tour."

After hanging up, both cousins scurried to their respective rooms and dressed for the day. A short time later, Candy, dressed in her turquoise felt poodle skirt, knocked on Ellen's door. "Ellen, I left Cutie home. He is so excited, and I did not want him to get worked up more if he saw Buttercup. My Pink Poodles and Bangs Brigade members keep calling. We're on the news. They are worried we can't handle the volume."

"Oh, Candy, I sure can understand why they are calling. But we are going to be just fine. We've cut off sales. Why don't you go back and get Cutie and head to your post. Let the ladies and dogs know it is going to be a wonderful tour and remind them to come here after the tour for a great celebration. By the way, you look just darling with your skirt and your bangs, and your anklets, and saddle shoes!"

Taking a deep breath, Ellen went back inside and said goodbye to Murph, who was headed to the tour start location where she was to meet her realtors who were serving as guides. She gathered Buttercup's leash and a bag of treats and met Sam in the alley. "Oh, thank you, Sam, for taking Buttercup to doggy daycare. She will have a great time there, and we and our neighbors won't have to listen to her bark all day."

Ellen went back in her house. Gave Sweetie Pie

a big kiss, grabbed her big straw hat and walked out her front door. She briskly walked the couple of blocks to the start of the tour. Oh, my, she exclaimed to herself when she saw all of the people lined up for the guided tour. Architect Betty Nobel was signing in each person. Murph and Javier gave their agents and the volunteer architects from the Colorado Association of Women Architects pink signs on tall sticks with numbers on them. People quickly assembled by the agent or architect who held the number of their ticket. Introductions were being made within each group. Then at 9 a.m. sharp the groups started out in different directions.

Ellen walked a short distance to another check-in table where Englewood's Community Relations Manager Karen Sanders and her friend Sarah Ferrell, a teacher at Englewood High School, sat. Small groups of people were coming up to them to check in and get a map of the self-guided walking tour. They explained that a member of the "Pink Poodles and Bangs Brigade" was stationed at each corner in case they got lost or wanted information about Mamie. They pointed to one of the brigade's members, Candy, with Cutie, who was standing a short distance away.

"Oh, my goodness," exclaimed one tour participant. "I used to have a skirt and shoes just like those and bangs when I was 8-years-old. Good grief. I remember wanting to dye our poodle named Huckleberry Hound pink, but my mom wouldn't let me. This tour is such fun. Where do we get the fudge and can you tell me, you know, which alley it was?"

Sarah said, "Along the route, you will come to tables draped with pink cloths and darling little kids and moms, if I might say so myself, with ruffled aprons on. As you know, we are selling fudge to get more

197

equipment for our schools, along with the help of many sponsors, including Evans Enterprises, Inc. who had the aprons made for us. We have a limited supply of fudge, so I'd suggest you buy some soon. A copy of Mamie's recipe comes with each plate."

"As far as the alley goes," Karen piped in, "we are asking everyone to be respectful of our citizens and these neighbors. Our police department will redirect anyone, except for locals, who try and go down the alley. We thank you for your consideration."

Just then, Cutie began to bark and the group headed down the sidewalk toward the little plump poodle.

The sun shined brightly throughout the day, highlighting the millions of pink blossoms on trees, many of which were over 60-years-old. Their sweet smell, along with the sun and delicious fudge, added to the feeling of a peaceful, easy and happy day.

Ellen, whose job was "chief point person and troubleshooter," smiled as she walked the streets. At one point she saw her neighbor Yah-Yah Girl. She was with Kelly and his brother Pat, holding a tour map. When they got to their other neighbor, Candy, she heard Yah-Yah Girl say, "Yah-yah, we knew all along that something strange was going on. I really feel sorry for his wife. I bet it was her that I heard scream that night." Looking up at Pat she went on, "It's really tough being a vet and all."

It was nearing 3 p.m. when Ellen started walking past Axle's house. He was in his front yard. Axle walked to the sidewalk to meet her. "So you got lots of people walking our neighborhood today, Ellen. BB told me you went and visited with her at her 'shop.' That took real guts, especially to ask her for a donation."

"You're right, Axle. It did take guts. After all,

I'm not the type that goes to the Teasing Tiger for lunch, you know!"

Both Axle and Ellen started to chuckle and then they broke out in an uproarious laughter, which seemed to melt the hate and anxiety away. "You know Axle, BB herself, is coming to my house around four to help us celebrate. You are more than welcome to pop in, too. We're going to have some great Mexican food from Lupita's."

"Thanks, Ellen. We'll see," Axle stated and started walking towards his garage.

When she got to the edge of his yard, Ellen noticed that both Joan and Lavonne were sitting on the porch at Brent's house. "Ellen," they called to her.

"Hi, ladies. I didn't expect to see either of you today, and I never ever thought I would see you both sitting together on this porch." Ellen walked into the yard and started up the steps to the front porch.

Both women stood up and when Ellen got to the porch, they immediately embraced in a group hug. Tears started flowing. "Oh, I am so sorry," Ellen said. "This is all so sad. I remember my mother talking about my dad, a World War II vet, screaming in the night. She called it shell shock. What he saw in that war tormented him until the day he died. I am truly sorry for your losses."

Lavonne came forward and said, "Oh, Ellen, thank you for understanding and not condemning. Joan and I came together over our mutual loss and now that Brent is gone, we have much to talk about. I do hope you will join us on this porch for a glass of wine soon."

"I would very much like to do that. Now, as you know, I must get back to my house. Goodbye, dear ladies."

Ellen hurried around the corner, past the old

farm houses to Emerald Street. She rushed past Candy's house on the corner, then Sam and Nancy's, and Annie's. Slightly out of breath, she bounded up the steps of her front porch and into her house. Murph met her at the door. "Where have you been, Ellen? The party is starting." Then, she took a look at her cousin and realized she had been crying. "Oh, lady, what is it?"

"I'll tell you later, Murph. Let me splash some water on my face and run a comb through my hair. I'll meet you in the backyard."

Ellen peeked out her back window before she went through the door to her patio. She heard Bill Haley and the Comets singing "Shake, Rattle and Roll." Green and -- who was that woman she wondered -- were doing the jitterbug. Tables had been set up on the lawn and she could smell the wonderful aromas of Mexican food, supplied by Lupita. BB was talking to Nancy, and Ellen realized the two women had known each other for a long time. Annie was sitting in a chair talking to dear Sam. I remember this song from when I was a little girl, but I bet Annie and her husband used to dance to it.

She slowly went out to her patio. Father Louie greeted her. "Oh Ellen, never in my wildest dreams or prayers did I think the murder would be solved so quickly. I am happy to tell you Hector's funeral is finally scheduled for Monday." Then he leaned in close and said, "The cops are going to let Jesus see it via Skype from his cell."

"You know, Father Louie, you were the one who put us on to solving it by telling me your hunch about the old warehouse district. Without that, the murder would not have been cracked."

Looking out on her lawn, she saw Mark McCoy and an attractive woman she guessed was his wife talking to Murph, Dan Green, Javier and the woman, who had been dancing with Green. She slowly walked to the group. McCoy saw her. "Well, Ellen. It is great to see you. What a wonderful event today. I'd like to introduce you to my wife, Lynne." Ellen shook hands with the attractive woman with sandy hair streaked with gray. "And I don't know if you know Willa Goddard. She's the superintendent at the jail Jesus calls home."

"Very funny, McCoy," Ellen said. She caught Murph winking at her

"Actually, Ellen, she will soon have a more impressive title as Mrs. Dan Green," Murph told her.

"Well, not really. I am planning on keeping my own name," Willa said as she slipped her hand into Dan's.

Murph jumped in, "At any rate, Javier and I are starting to look for a new home for them. After today's tour, I think they might be partial to the mid-century architecture here in Olde Englewood. I know Dan wanted a quick getaway to the mountains and Highway 285 certainly will meet that hope. But now, I must leave you and go take a commanding position on your patio, my dear Ellen, and start the acknowledgements for today's great tour. Besides, I am famished. Let's get this over so we can eat!"

With that announcement, she went up to the patio. Someone turned up the music and Dean Martin started singing "That's Amore." When the song stopped, everyone was gathered around the patio looking at Murph.

"What an amazing day," Murph proclaimed as she began her speech. The audience applauded and hooted. "You know, my cousin Ellen, who's hosting this party and co-chairing the Pink Blossoms Neighborhood and Garden Tour, and I are fifth-generation Colorado natives. And I bet Ellen would agree with me, Colorado days don't come any better than today. Isn't this sunshine outrageous!"

The crowd applauded.

"Ellen and I both remember when Mamie was First Lady. And yep, we both had bangs, and yep, our mothers made us turquoise blue felt skirts with a pink poodle appliqué. Don't you think our Pink Poodles and Bangs Brigade was the best?" Applause erupted. "Please take a bow, ladies." And I want to acknowledge the leader, one of Ellen's neighbors, Candy Wallace. Did you know they are all nurses? That's one of the great things about this neighborhood. So many wonderful hospitals within miles of each other."

Murph continued by introducing and acknowledging all of the committee members and sponsors. When she got to Lupita, she said, "Ellen and I recently visited Lupita at her fine Mexican restaurant. I said to Lupita "Do you remember my cousin Ellen, who used to try so hard to keep up with us playing Queen of the Mountain? She replied, 'Oh, my, don't tell me this is the skinny tall kid with the pale red braids! Really?' I said, "The one and only – and here we are some 65 years later and none of us have scabs and band aides on our knees and elbows." The audience laughed and Lupita grinned.

"We did this tour today because we all know developers," loud boos interrupted her, "would love to scrape these well-built sensible houses and put up condos that would reach the sky. As John Denver sang in his song "Rocky Mountain High," 'More people, more scars upon this land.' We wanted to bring awareness to this lovely architecture, charming area and to a woman who called it home, Mamie Dowd Eisenhower. I think we did that today!" Murph's next words were drowned out by applause and hooting.

When it quieted down, she went on, "Yes, we

did! And I can tell you, thanks to Mamie and her fudge recipe, and the mothers and fathers and kids in this audience who all whipped up lots of batches and sold them today, we made heaps of money for new equipment for Englewood schools, over $40,000!" The crowd started singing, "That's Amore."

Murph concluded, and now one more announcement. "On this wonderful note and because you guys can sing so well, I am announcing my retirement and warning you very soon there won't be any fish left in the Frying Pan River!"

Ellen went up to her cousin and gave her a big hug. "One more thing," Ellen said to the group. "As a little token on my appreciation for all the work the committee put in and the efforts of our sponsors –all women, mind you – I have a little pink shimmering drawstring evening bag I knitted for you, using a pattern from the 1950s. However, unlike the women back then, you don't have to wait until that special date to wear it. For example, I bet Murph will fill hers with fishing gear, you know hooks and flies and fishing line."

Clapping erupted and soon everyone was gathered around them, wishing Murph a great retirement and thanking them and the committee and the sponsors for all their work.

Over the heads of the crowd, Ellen got a glimpse of Dungaree. He was sitting on her bench in her rose garden, stroking Buttercup's head. She thought oh, that's right, Sam told me doggie daycare closed at four. How strange. Buttercup is not running all over the place and trying to eat all the food. She seems so content. Ellen looked a little closer at Dungaree. He seemed content, too. He caught her eye and winked.

Suddenly, BB's words came back to her, "Even tough ol' broads need a little love. I'd be careful, Ms.

Lane. You're pretty and skinny. I would think there would be a "Mrs." in front of Lane. Like I said, we all need a little love."

And to think I met him in my alley, and he likes to play golf at my very favorite course right here in Colorado, not far from the Frying Pan River.

Ellen winked back.

MAMIE'S FUDGE RECIPE

4 ½ c. sugar
1/8 teaspoon salt
2 tablespoons butter
12-oz. can evaporated milk
12-oz. semi-sweet chocolate chips
12-oz. milk chocolate or
   German-sweet chocolate
14 oz. marshmallow cream
2 c. walnuts

Butter a 13X9-in. pan In a large heat-proof bowl, combine chocolate chips & marshmallow crème. In alarge saucepan over medium heat, combine the milk, sugar and butter. Bring to a boil, stirring constantly.

Boil and stir for 5 minutes. Pour over chocolate mixture; stir until chocolate is melted and mixture is smooth and creamy. Stir in walnuts. Pour into pan. Cover and refrigerate until firm. Cut into 1-inch squares. Store in an airtight container in the refrigerator.

ABOUT THE AUTHOR

Born in 1947, Elizabeth's parents nicknamed her Reddy Kilowatt, after the famous utility company mascot, who also had red hair. She has been igniting the world ever since.

She is one of a few women who graduated from the University of Colorado's graduate School of Business in 1973. Before retiring, she headed up marketing/public relations departments for the American Red Cross, American Cancer Society, a Novartis generic pharmaceuticals company, and the University of Colorado Hospital.

For this book, her experience in obtaining a major grant for the Mamie Doud Eisenhower Library in Broomfield, Colorado, and guiding the opening of the historic Eisenhower Suite in the historic Building 500 at the University of Colorado Anschutz Medical Center gave her a keen understanding of President Eisenhower and his wife Mamie, who grew up in Denver.

After retiring, Elizabeth, a Colorado native and old house lover, founded Denver's Old House Society. The organization's main efforts were guided walking tours and an old house fair.

Elizabeth has authored four books. Her blog, "Ladies-of-a-Certain-Age," is read by women throughout the country and several foreign countries.

She has three children and four grandchildren. Currently, she resides on Colorado's Western Slope with her Airedale Terrier, and her tuxedo cat, Katie Lane Lynch, named after Elizabeth's great-great-grandmother, an early Colorado pioneer. She enjoys gardening, knitting, hiking and playing pickleball.

Made in the USA
Columbia, SC
20 April 2021